JERRY MAHONEY

My Rotten
Stepbrother Ruined
ALADDIN

STONE ARCH BOOKS
a capstone imprint

My Rotten Stepbrother Ruined Fairy Tales is published by
Stone Arch Books, A Capstone Imprint
1710 Roe Crest Drive
North Mankato, Minnesota 56003
www.mycapstone.com

Text © 2018 Jerry Mahoney
Illustrations © 2018 Stone Arch Books

Library of Congress Cataloging-in-Publication Data
Names: Mahoney, Jerry, 1971- author. | Bitskoff, Aleksei, author.
Title: My rotten stepbrother ruined Aladdin / by Jerry Mahoney ; illustrated
by Aleksei Bitskoff.
Description: North Mankato, Minnesota : Stone Arch Books, a Capstone
imprint, 2017. | Series: My rotten stepbrother ruined fairy tales |
Summary: Maddie's birthday party has an Aladdin theme, but when
her stepbrother's separate birthday gets ruined, and he does not get the
hoverboard he craves, he deliberately breaks the Aladdin story, sucking
both of them into the world of the fairy tale — and while he gets to be
Aladdin and find the genie, Maddie is stuck as a camel.
Identifiers: LCCN 2017003928| ISBN 9781496544643 (library binding) |
ISBN 9781496544681 (pbk.) | ISBN 9781496544803 (ebook (pdf))
Subjects: LCSH: Aladdin (Tale)—Juvenile fiction. | Magic—Juvenile fiction. |
Jinn—Juvenile fiction. | Stepbrothers—Juvenile fiction. | Brothers
and sisters—Juvenile fiction. | CYAC: Fairy tales—Fiction. | Characters
in literature—Fiction. | Magic—Fiction. | Genies—Fiction. | Stepbrothers
Fiction. | Brothers and sisters—Fiction. | LCGFT: Fairy tales.
Classification: LCC PZ7.1.M3467 Mz 2017 | DDC 813.6 [Fic]—dc23
LC record available at https://lccn.loc.gov/2017003928

Illustrations: Aleksei Bitskoff

Designer: Ashlee Suker

Printed in China.
010375F17

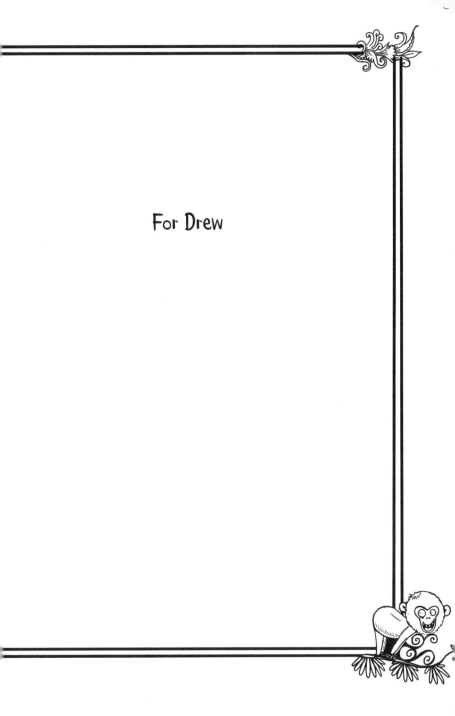

For Drew

For once, Maddie didn't need her alarm clock to wake her up. She rose with the sun, perky and full of life, and she got out of bed without a single groan of protest. In a matter of minutes, she had showered, brushed her hair, and put on her favorite dress: the one with the blue floral pattern and the bright red sash. She sat down at the kitchen table to find that her dad had already whipped her up a plate of strawberry waffles, her favorite. She wasn't normally a morning person, but this was a morning worth waking up for: her birthday. It had always been her favorite day of the year.

"Haffy birfday to me," sang a familiar voice, coming from down the hall. "Haffy BIRFFFFFFFFFDAY TOOOO MEEEEEEE!"

Maddie groaned. Today was also her rotten stepbrother, Holden's, birthday. He had annoyingly been born on the same day she had, and now that their parents were married, Maddie had to share her special day with her least favorite person on Earth. Even as he brushed his teeth, he couldn't help singing a garbled, off-key version of "Happy Birthday" in his own honor. As she took her first bite of waffle, Maddie seriously considered using her birthday wish to make tomorrow come ASAP.

She tried to remind herself that Holden would be gone for most of the day, off zip-lining at an adventure park with three of his goony friends. So at least it would be a quiet birthday. Then, that night, she was going to have the most awesome sleepover party ever, and their parents had made Holden promise not to ruin it.

This was the upside of Maddie's dad remarrying. He never liked parties himself, but his new wife, Carol, lived for them. In the old days, Maddie's dad would blow up a few balloons and stick some candles in an ice cream cake from the grocery store. Everything was done at the last minute. But Carol had been planning for months. She and Maddie decided on an *Aladdin* theme, and Carol had gone all-out. She helped Maddie make gummy magic lamps, sleeping bags that looked like flying carpets, and veils that said, "Happy birthday, Maddie!", which they would wear while belly dancing to some Middle Eastern music.

Originally, Maddie had resisted choosing a fairy tale for her party's theme. Ever since her stepbrother came into her life, her love of fairy tales had caused her a lot of aggravation. It started when Holden pointed out the plot holes in *Cinderella*. The next thing they knew, the story had completely changed, and the prince proposed to one of the wicked stepsisters. Then, Maddie and Holden got sucked into a tablet computer. They found themselves in the world of the story, Maddie as a stepsister and Holden as a palace guard. The only way they could get back home was to give Cinderella back her happily ever after, and it wasn't easy.

You might think Holden would've learned his lesson after that, but then he started picking apart *Beauty and the Beast*, and the Beast got thrown in jail for kidnapping. Holden and Maddie had to rescue him before he got his head chopped off. It was while they were in that story that they learned they'd been cursed by a mixed-up fairy named Resplenda. She wanted to teach Holden a lesson for being such a brat, so as long as he kept snarking on fairy tales, he and Maddie were going to keep getting sent in to fix them.

Maddie had to admit, though, there was something fun about getting to live in a fairy tale for a little while.

Taking a quick trip into *Aladdin* actually sounded kind of cool, especially if she got to be the glamorous Princess Nazeerah. She'd live in a towering palace overlooking the mystical deserts of Arabia and be wooed by the handsome young rebel Aladdin. There would be magic and wonder and flying carpet rides by moonlight. She could think of worse ways to spend her twelfth birthday.

There was another great thing about throwing an *Aladdin* party: it drove Holden nuts. He wanted nothing to do with the decorating, the games, the food. Whenever Maddie and Carol would start talking about it, he would run out of the room with his hands over his ears, shouting, "Worst party idea ever!" Normally, he was the one trying to get under Maddie's skin, so it was a nice change for her to be irritating him for once. In fact, she decided to confront him directly about the story. If he had any plot holes to point out, she wanted him to do it before her friends arrived.

She caught him just as he was pulling on his jacket to leave for zip-lining. "Go ahead," she said, arms folded, prepared for his trash talk.

"What? Oh, sorry. Am I supposed to wish you a happy birthday?"

"Not that," Maddie whispered. "*Aladdin*. I'm sure you're dying to tell me what's wrong with the story, so why not do it now and get it over with?"

Holden shook his head vigorously. "Oh no!" he said. "I've learned my lesson. Every time I talk smack on a fairy tale, I end up having to hang out with princesses and go to balls and junk like that. Let me make one thing very clear." He seemed to be speaking more to the sky now than to Maddie, as if he were hoping to be heard by Resplenda, the fairy who cursed them. "I have no complaints with *Aladdin*!"

Maddie sighed in relief, or was it disappointment? If Holden wasn't going to mock *Aladdin*, that meant her decorations were as close as she'd come to being in the story. It looked like this was just going to be an ordinary birthday after all.

"Besides," Holden added, "our parents hate it when we fight, and I'm not doing anything to mess up my chances of getting a you-know-what."

She knew what. Everyone knew what Holden wanted for his birthday. Every five seconds for the last six months, he'd reminded anyone who would listen that he absolutely had to have a hoverboard or he'd just die. Specifically, he wanted the iJet ZX-4500 Ultra Hoverjammer from Sizzletech Industries of Sandusky, Ohio. In black and hot pink. With a skull on it. He had said it so many times that Maddie had it memorized.

He felt like he had pretty much mastered his skateboard. If there was anything holding him back from world domination, it was gravity. With a hoverboard, he'd be unstoppable. He could do infinite spins in the air, pull off grabs twenty feet from the ground, and perform grinds off helicopter blades and skyscraper antennae. He was so stoked for the hoverboard he had convinced himself he was getting, that he cleared off shelf space in his room. He planned to keep it in the prime spot between the mountain of unwashed gym socks and the fish tank he used to keep his frogs in until they died.

"Hoverboards are so dangerous," Maddie said. "People get sprains, broken bones, and permanent scars from them, all over their body. Sometimes, the boards just all of a sudden burst into flames!"

"I know!" Holden exclaimed. "Doesn't it sound awesome?"

Just then, Maddie's dad came out of his bedroom and saw them talking in the hallway.

"Uh-oh," he said, instinctively. "What are you two fighting about?"

"Not a thing!" Holden said, putting his arm around Maddie. Maddie gasped at the affection. Holden had never willingly made physical contact with her before. "Just sharing a nice morning chat with my birthday buddy." Holden flashed a charming smile, then headed out to the car, whistling "Happy Birthday."

"You two are getting along?" Maddie's dad said, in awe. "Is this a birthday present for me?"

"Oh, I'm sure he'll be back to his obnoxious old self in no time," Maddie said.

"Just take it easy on him," her dad replied. "You know today is extra tough on him."

"Why? Because he has to share his birthday with me?"

"No," her dad said. "I meant it's his first without his dad."

Maddie had forgotten. A few months ago, Holden's dad got a job in Germany, and since then, Holden had barely heard from him. He was very busy working, and given the time difference between New Jersey and Europe, they were rarely able to chat. Of course, Holden didn't ever share his feelings, but Maddie's dad had let her know that he'd been taking the separation very hard.

"Look, don't mention anything to him. Just try to get along with him for the rest of the day."

Maddie nodded. Now she was hoping Holden actually would get his hoverboard. Even a creep like him deserved to have a nice birthday.

Soon, Holden and Greg were off to the adventure park, and Maddie and Carol got to work turning their living room into the mystical kingdom of Arabia. Carol had scoured the Internet for *Aladdin*-themed craft ideas, and together they set the scene for the slumber party. Maddie constructed a life-size camel out of balloons, while Carol made a festooned elephant from garbage bags and a throw rug. Together, they built an oasis out of a kiddie pool and papier-mâché palm trees.

Maddie enjoyed having someone so crafty in the family. The most creative thing her dad ever did was to spell out *Go Team!* in cocktail wieners for his annual Super Bowl party.

It was only a few minutes after he left that Holden's tablet began to vibrate. Maddie peeked at it and saw that Holden's dad was trying to video chat with him. He was going to be so disappointed that he missed the call!

When Maddie's friends arrived, the mini replica of Arabia in the living room earned their highest rating: five OMGs. Maddie's friend Tasha Simmons even called it "the coolest party ever," to which Abby Chou enthusiastically replied, "Uh-huh!" Maddie and Carol shared a secret high-five as the girls tried the chocolate chip hummus. Success!

Suddenly, the front door flew open, and a grouchy voice rang through the house. "Worst birthday ever!" Holden was home. And he was soaking wet.

Maddie had been so caught up in decorating that she hadn't even noticed it was pouring rain outside. "How was zip-lining?" she asked, timidly.

"Horrible!" Holden griped, as he took his first look at the decorations. "Almost as horrible as all of this garbage!"

"Well, I have some good news. Your dad tried to video chat with you."

"How is that good news? I can't call him back now." He looked at the clock. "It's after midnight in Germany! It's not even my birthday there anymore." He shoved the balloon camel out of his way and stomped upstairs angrily.

Maddie's dad shook his head, sadly. "The storm hit just as we got there. It was too windy for the zip lines, and too rainy for everything else. I took the guys to lunch, but they were pretty bummed out."

Once again, Maddie felt bad for her stepbrother. As jerky as he was, it wasn't right for anyone to be sad on their birthday. She decided she would do something nice for him, to cheer him up.

First, though, she had some guests to entertain. Maddie's dad surprised them all by dressing up like a genie. "I will grant you three wishes," he said in a deep voice as Maddie and her friends giggled. "One, for stuffed-crust pizza; two, to watch a PG-13 movie; and three, to stay up until midnight." The girls cheered.

There were four pizzas. The first one to go was the veggie pizza. Then, the pepperoni. Then, the plain. Then, still hungry, the girls opened up the last box, which was pineapple, anchovies, and no cheese.

Holden's favorite.

Maddie couldn't imagine anyone but her weird stepbrother even liking such a freakish combination of toppings, but her friends were hungry enough that they tore right through it. Slice by slice, the pie disappeared before her eyes. Maddie couldn't bear to think of Holden not getting any pizza on his own birthday, so she quietly slid three slices onto a paper plate and snuck away from the table.

She found Holden in the kitchen, poking through the refrigerator for a snack. "Thought you might like this," she said, holding out the weird pizza slices.

Holden didn't turn around. He didn't even acknowledge her.

"Look, I'm sorry your birthday was ruined," she said.

Holden still didn't acknowledge Maddie. Now, she was starting to get annoyed. "Look, I saved you some pizza. The least you can do is—"

Finally, Holden turned around, pulling earbuds out of his ear. He was listening to music on his tablet. "Sorry, were you talking? I cranked up the new Hashtag Number Sign album."

Hashtag Number Sign was Holden's favorite band. He'd begged his mom to let him go to their concert, but she said he was too young. "Ugh, I don't know why you like that band," Maddie said. "They're so loud they drive me crazy."

"Funny enough, that's why I like them. Plus, they help drown out all the high-pitched shrieking from your party."

"Come on. It's not that bad!" Maddie laughed.

"I think slumber parties stink big time, but I'm glad you're having fun."

"Really?" Maddie was stunned to hear Holden say something so kind. Maybe all the time they spent together in fairy tales had made him more thoughtful.

Holden shrugged. "Not really, but I told my mom I'd be nice to you, and she's upstairs wrapping my present right now, so . . . y'know."

Maddie smiled. "Well, I think hoverboards stink big time, but I hope you get one."

"Aw, thanks," Holden said, ripping off a chunk of pizza with his teeth. As Maddie turned to leave, their parents entered. Carol held something behind her back. "You weren't kidding," Carol said to Greg. "They really are getting along."

Holden flashed a charming grin. "Why, of course! We're like brother and sister."

Maddie struggled to control her impulse to roll her eyes. She knew it was all an act so he could get the hoverboard.

Carol smiled. "Since you're in such a good mood, maybe now's a good time to give you something."

Holden stepped forward. "Why, whatever could it be? A birthday present of some kind? Well, I don't think there's anything I want, is there?"

Carol sighed. "Honey, I know you wanted a hoverboard, but—"

Holden stopped smiling. "But what?" he said. His voice was sharp with anger.

Greg decided to step in and deliver the bad news. "We decided they're just too dangerous. Broken bones, blood, permanent scars. And the way they sometimes burst into flames!"

"That's why I want one!" Holden protested.

"Well, I think you're really going to love what we got you!" Carol held out a small box, barely the size of her hand. "Open it."

"What is that?" Holden said, stepping forward. He quietly took the box out of his mom's hand, flipped it over, and inspected it. All at once, the anger came rushing back to his face. "If it's not a hoverboard," he said, "it's garbage!"

He threw the present across the room, into the trash can, where it landed on top of a bunch of pizza crusts and soda cups. Then, he bolted out of the room.

"Holden Benjamin!" Carol shouted.

Whoa, Maddie thought. She must really be mad if she used his middle name.

"Let him go," Greg said, resting his hand on Carol's shoulder.

Maddie couldn't believe they were going to let him run away, so she followed him instead. When she got to the living room, she found him standing in the middle of her friends, ranting angrily. "I hope you're enjoying your miserable party!" he said. "Because let me tell you what's wrong with *Aladdin*. What kind of guy gets three wishes and uses them to become a prince and to have some princess fall in love with him? No guy I've ever known. Being a prince sounds lame. No thanks. And if the genie's been in the bottle for tens of thousands of years, why isn't he a Neanderthal? He should be talking like someone with a primitive brain, like, 'Duh, what you wish?' Most of all, though, any halfway-intelligent person knows to exploit the three-wish loophole."

"What's that?" Maddie asked.

"The loophole is that you can use one of your wishes to wish for infinite wishes, then the genie is yours forever!"

"But that's mean!" Maddie said.

"So?" Holden shrugged. "Genies aren't people. They're made to serve us. Any genie would probably be thrilled to have you wish for infinite wishes."

Carol and Greg entered to see what Holden was shouting about. He looked directly at them. "And once you wish for infinite wishes, your second wish should be for no parents!" He charged upstairs, leaping three steps at a time so he'd be gone as fast as possible. The last thing everyone heard was the sound of his door slamming, followed by loud rock music blasting. Holden was officially calling an end to this birthday.

Chapter 2

There was no sign of Holden for the rest of Maddie's party. He wasn't there for belly dancing or Pin the Hump on the Camel, and he wanted nothing to do with the movie they watched, about the two sick teenagers who fell in love. (Maddie and her teary friends went through three full boxes of tissues during that one.) When he failed to come down for cake, Maddie knew he must be in serious mope mode.

Carol had made each of the birthday kids their own cake, just the way they asked for it. Holden's had black frosting and a scary clown face on it. Instead of *Happy birthday*, the icing spelled out *Holden rulz*. But he refused to come down to blow out the candles.

"I guess we'll just save this until he's feeling up for it," Carol said, putting Holden's cake in the fridge.

"Looks like your birthday wish already came true, Maddie!" Tasha joked as Maddie leaned in to blow out her candles. "Your stepbrother disappeared!"

All the girls laughed, but Maddie felt a pit in her stomach. As much as Holden drove her nuts, it pained her to think he was spending his birthday sulking in his bedroom, alone. She knew exactly how it felt to want something and to be told she couldn't have it. When she was little, she begged her dad for a fancy doll that he said was just too expensive. Then, there was the home makeover kit that her dad wouldn't buy her because he didn't think she was old enough for makeup.

Maddie took a deep breath and settled on the perfect wish. *I wish Holden could get everything he wants for his birthday,* she thought to herself, and with one big exhale, she wiped out all twelve candles on her cake.

By 11:00, Maddie's dad had changed out of his genie costume and into his pajamas.

"Now I get to grant my own wish," he cracked, "for some peace and quiet!"

As he and Carol went upstairs, Maddie whispered an apology to her friends. "Ugh, my dad's jokes are the worst!"

Now on their own, the girls celebrated their freedom by making microwave popcorn, dimming the living room lights, and telling ghost stories.

"It was a night just like this one, in a town not far away," Diana Lopez whispered, shining a flashlight on her face. "The moon was full, the air was still, and it was one hundred years to the day that the worst tragedy ever in the town had happened."

Everyone leaned in to hear the gruesome tale, except Maddie, who was distracted by a faint light coming from upstairs, in Holden's bedroom. He was still awake, probably still miserable. As she watched her friends huddle together in fear, she knew just what would cheer up her stepbrother — the chance to sneak in and scare them. All he'd have to do is hide until a tense moment in one of the stories and then jump out and scream, "Boo!" It would actually be kind of funny, so she quietly slipped away to give him the idea.

She made her way upstairs to his bedroom, but before she even had a chance to knock on the door, he croaked, "Go away!"

"But I have an idea," Maddie said. "You could really freak all the girls out."

"Not interested," Holden said. "Good night!"

Maddie sighed. "I'm sorry about the hoverboard. I still think they should've just bought you one."

"I should've asked my dad," Holden replied. "He would've gotten me one."

Maddie's heart sank. She had forgotten about Holden's father. Not hearing from him all day certainly wasn't helping Holden's mood.

"Come on, we're telling ghost stories," Maddie said. "I'll bet you know some good ones."

Holden responded by turning on loud rock music. He obviously didn't want her sympathy, and he didn't want to be cheered up. He just wanted to be alone.

Even though she knew he couldn't hear her, Maddie whispered, "Happy birthday" through the door. Then she turned around and went back to her party.

Holden couldn't quite make out anything the singer was saying. He wasn't really singing, actually. He was making this deep, guttural scream that shook the walls. Holden thought he heard the word *annihilate*. Maybe there was a *devastation* in the lyrics, too. It may not have made much sense, but it was the perfect music to be angry to.

It was rock music, and it was awesome.

Holden jumped on his bed and nodded his head to the beat. If his mom wouldn't let him go to a Hashtag Number

Sign concert, he could at least pretend he was at one. This band kicked butt.

Pretty soon, there was a pounding on the wall. "Holden, headphones, please!" his mom shouted. It was a tired, weak shout. His mom would be an awful rock singer.

Holden strapped on his headphones. Being angry wasn't as fun with headphones on, but that was his only choice right now. It really was the worst birthday ever.

All he wanted was to go to bed and put this birthday behind him, but he couldn't just yet. He watched the clock, waiting for it to turn midnight. As miserable as it was, he was going to have to spend the entire rest of this horrible day awake.

At midnight, it would be a new day here in Middle Grove, New Jersey. Even better, it would be 6 a.m. in Germany, and that meant his dad would be waking up. It would be the perfect time to video chat with him on his tablet.

His dad would understand how he was feeling. He'd think it was totally lame that his mom didn't get him a hoverboard. He'd probably have one express shipped overseas that day. His dad was cool.

11:59. Holden imagined his dad, probably snoring loudly in a tiny German cottage as the sun came up over the

Alps. Was he wearing *lederhosen*? Probably. That's what people wore to bed in Germany. Any second now, his alarm would go off, and he would wake up, ready to talk to his son.

Holden picked up the tablet to shut off the music. That's when he noticed that the screen was no longer showing the cover of Hashtag Number Sign's album. It was showing an illustration from *Aladdin*. It was the one thing that could've made this birthday worse.

This was what happened after he criticized a fairy tale. First, the eBook appeared on his tablet screen. Then, he noticed how the story had changed, and finally, he and Maddie got sucked into the book to fix things.

Not this time.

He turned the tablet over, slid it across his desk, then dumped all his dirty laundry on top of it. He wanted nothing to do with another lousy fairy tale, especially not on the worst birthday of his life. Maybe he'd get a new tablet. A different brand, a new Wi-Fi network. He'd delete the eBook app. There had to be a way around this curse.

That's when he noticed the clock switching from 11:59 to 12:00. It was the time he'd been waiting for all day. Right now, in Germany, his dad was waking up.

If he wanted to talk to him, he was going to have to look at his tablet again. Sighing deeply, he dug the device out from under his dirty socks and glanced at the screen.

It was still showing *Aladdin*, of course. Holden figured he might as well see what damage he'd done to the story, so he began swiping his way through the pages. It didn't seem that different at first. There was a picture of Aladdin discovering the lamp, just like always. Then came a picture of the genie rolling his eyes, which seemed a little out of character, but nothing major. He turned the next page, and what he saw shocked him so much, he dropped the tablet.

It was a drawing of Aladdin riding a hoverboard.

That's my wish, Holden thought. It didn't take him long to figure out what that meant. *If we go into the story, I'll be Aladdin!*

Holden stared at the picture for a long time. Aladdin was hoverboarding — and at the same time chugging an energy drink and eating a pineapple/anchovy/no cheese pizza. No doubt about it. That was him — and he was having the time of his life.

A devious grin broke out on Holden's face. He tucked the tablet under his arm and headed out into the hallway.

All the girls were sleeping downstairs. They looked so silly, with their messy hair, droopy eyes, and drool dripping out of their mouths. A couple of them were snoring. He wanted to record the whole thing and put it online for his friends to see. Maddie's friends would be so embarrassed. But there was something more important he had to do first.

He found Maddie and placed the tablet beside her on her sleeping bag. Then, very gently, he slid her left hand over and rested it on the screen.

"Once upon a time," he said, and in an instant, his body began to tingle and shrink.

Maddie's eyes sprung open as she realized what was going on. "Holden?" she said. She watched him get sucked into the tablet's glowing screen. "Why would you—?"

With a whoosh, Maddie was swept up as well. She hovered briefly over her friends before getting sucked into the tablet screen. A couple of the girls stirred at the sound and the flash of light, but all of them settled down and fell back into a deep sleep, unaware that Holden, Maddie, and the tablet had all disappeared from the living room.

Chapter
3

Maddie found herself floating against an all-white background. She was still half-asleep, which was why it took her so long to realize she'd been here before. Yes, she knew this place. It was the blank page of a book, waiting to be filled in with words and images.

Why had Holden brought them here? She had felt him move her hand onto his tablet screen, and she had heard him say the words, "Once upon a time . . ." He knew as well as she did that was what caused them to get sucked into fairy tales. He had specifically said he didn't want anything to do with *Aladdin*. Now, there he was, floating next to her, grinning like a total doofus. It didn't make any sense.

Then came the words *palace, desert, cave*.

The scene behind them filled in with the sights of *Aladdin* — the booby-trapped cave, the Arabian Desert, Nazeerah's palace. As she watched the scenery burst to life, Maddie started to get excited.

Whatever her stepbrother's reasons might be, she was going to be part of one of her favorite stories. At least, a part of a mixed-up version of it. As words flew over Maddie's head, she tried to remember what Holden's gripe with the story was. He didn't think Aladdin would use one of his wishes to become a prince just so he could marry Princess Nazeerah. Was that it? Big deal.

That would be an easy fix, especially if she got to be Nazeerah. All she had to do was marry Aladdin against her father's wishes, and they'd live happily ever after. Then, Maddie would be back home at her slumber party with a really cool adventure under her belt.

Maddie looked over, but Holden was already gone. She had been so lost in thought that she hadn't seen whom he turned into in the story. That would make it much harder to track him down. Well, as Nazeerah, she would have a lot of royal guards and helpers at her service. She would use everything at her disposal to find her stepbrother, just so he could be there when Nazeerah and Aladdin got married, and she could rub his face in it.

Words were flying by with great speed by now, and the world of the story was truly taking shape. There was a mighty palace, a maze-like shopping bazaar, flowing sand dunes, and a gorgeous pink and blue Arabian sky. Maddie kept her eyes open in anticipation of the word *Nazeerah*, which would surely be flying over her head any moment now.

She saw more words zoom past: *lamp, carpet, genie.*

Then, finally, the one she had been waiting for: *Nazeerah.*

She smiled as it rocketed toward her, but her smile soon disappeared, as the word kept going, fading behind her into the story.

Too bad. So if she wasn't Nazeerah, who would she be?

Only one word remained, flying at her so fast she couldn't quite make it out. Was that a C? An A? What could it be? She squinted, and soon the word came to a stop, just above her head. Did that say what she thought it did? No, that was impossible.

It almost looked like it said *camel.*

Chapter 4

Maddie found herself on the outskirts of a bustling shopping bazaar. Merchants shouted sales pitches to everyone passing by. "Buy my rugs!" "Make me an offer!" "Top quality wagon wheels!" They were desperate to get the attention of any customer in the area, but Maddie noticed something very strange. None of them were calling to her. She gazed around, but not a single one of these eager salespeople even made eye contact with her. Was she invisible or something?

She felt her jaw moving up and down in a circular motion. Inside her mouth, a sticky substance sloshed around and around. It had a strange taste, a little sour. Was it yogurt? No, it was thicker, more like oatmeal. Next, she noticed an incredibly foul odor in the air. Whoever she was, it smelled like she hadn't bathed in weeks. That would have to be her first order of business in this fairy tale: finding somewhere to wash up. She wouldn't be able to bear the smell much longer.

Whatever she was eating, it didn't taste very good, so Maddie decided to swallow it and get it over with. Whew. Now, maybe she could finally look around and figure out who she was.

Before she got a chance, though, she felt her stomach churning. It was the feeling she always had just before she threw up. Sure enough, she began to heave, and then the food she'd been chewing came bursting back up her esophagus into her mouth. Gross! What a horrible way to start a fairy tale, by puking her guts out in front of a bunch of strangers. As the food came back up her throat and dribbled out of her mouth, she expected everyone to look over at her, disgusted, but still, no one noticed.

Stranger still, she found herself chewing again, as if by instinct. Her mouth started moving up and down, around and around. She thought back to the word that stopped above her head: *camel.*

She looked over her shoulder, and sure enough, she saw a furry brown hump bulging out of her back.

She *was* a camel!

That meant that what she was eating wasn't oatmeal. She was chewing cud!

Yuck! Maddie spat out the contents of her mouth, and for the first time, the people passing by noticed her.

"Disgusting!" an old woman jeered, stepping around the puddle Maddie had made on the ground.

Maddie felt her breath quicken. This was terrible! She wanted to be Princess Nazeerah, but instead, she was an animal — a smelly, spitty animal who, as far as she knew, didn't play any role in the story of *Aladdin*. How would she ever give the tale back its happily ever after now? How would she get the characters in the story to interact with her? How would she get the horrible taste of throw-up out of her mouth?

She took some deep breaths and tried to calm herself down. She could do this. First, she would have to find Holden and come up with a plan. Surely, he was somewhere nearby. He was probably another camel.

"Bwehh-ehh-ehhhhhh!" came a strange sound from nearby. It was almost like the sound of someone trying to start the engine on a really old car. But there were no cars in *Aladdin*.

"Bwehh-ehh-ehhhhhh!" she heard again. When she looked in the direction of the sound, she saw a group of camels tied to a fence just outside the bazaar. They seemed to be calling to her.

"Bwehh-ehh-ehhhhhh!"

She began to walk toward the camels, but her wobbly knees gave out. She belly flopped onto the sand, her head crashing in the dirt.

Now people were noticing her. "Look at that weird camel!" they said. "What's wrong with it?"

Maddie staggered back to her feet. If it was possible for a camel to blush, she was pretty sure that's what she was doing. She wasn't used to walking on four legs. She wasn't even sure how.

She observed the way the other camels moved and did her best to copy them. Front left foot, back right foot, front right foot, back left foot. Repeat.

She took a careful step forward, then another and another. It wasn't so hard once she got used to it. Maddie started to feel really good about her ability to walk as a camel. Thankfully, people stopped paying attention to her, and she made her way over to the other camels.

She scanned their faces. It was hard to tell one from the other. She remembered from the other fairy tales that she would be able to recognize Holden's face when she saw him. But was that still true if he wasn't human? One of the camels in the cluster had a very distinct expression on his face. One of his eyebrows was cocked, and one side of his mouth was curled upward. She couldn't be sure, but it almost looked like he was smirking sarcastically! That had to be him!

"Holden?" Maddie asked, stepping closer to the sarcastic camel. She was relieved to find she could still speak normally. "Is that you?"

Pfft! The next thing Maddie knew, she felt a blast of warm, gummy liquid in her face. She recognized the smell and the taste instantly.

It was cud. The camel spat at her!

"Hey!" Maddie said. "That's not nice!"

PFFT! Now, all the other camels spat in her face as well. "Ew!" She realized they were probably pretty freaked out to see one of their own talking. Okay, so maybe Holden wasn't a camel after all. Maddie walked away from the group, wondering how she'd find him now.

Her thinking was interrupted by a loud, magnificent trumpeting sound. The people around her scurried and cleared the road, and a series of thundering footsteps shook the ground. Thump, thump, thump, thump!

Maddie looked down the road and saw a huge caravan making its way toward them. Guards with long, curved swords marched in their direction, followed by an entourage of camels and important-looking people. The animals were all laden down with goods from the bazaar — silk tablecloths, fine china, blossoming floral arrangements.

At the rear was a mighty elephant, on top of which a woman rode. The spectators waved to her eagerly. Some giggled, some gasped, all of them in awe as the woman came into view. She waved back to the people and smiled at them, her long, black hair falling straight down her back. "Farewell!" she shouted. "Thank you for everything! I loved meeting you all!"

She was gorgeous — flawless, even — and so regal. There was no doubt in Maddie's mind who this was.

It could only be Princess Nazeerah.

Maddie stood there, staring at her in awe, as the elephant stomped closer and closer to her. Finally, one of the swordsmen ran up to Maddie and began nudging her. "You crazy camel!" he shouted. "Move!"

Maddie realized that if she didn't move immediately, she'd be crushed under the elephant's gigantic foot. Alarmed, she sprang quickly into action and tried to run away. She was in such a hurry that she forgot everything she learned about walking as a camel, and she felt her knees begin to wobble again. OOF! She belly flopped into a sand dune.

She was stuck there, sprawled out in the desert, with no time to stand back up, as Princess Nazeerah's elephant headed right for her.

Chapter 5

Holden thought for a moment he was back on a blank page, except instead of everything around him being white, it was completely black. He couldn't see a thing, not even his own hand in front of his face.

He started to get some disturbing thoughts, like what if he was surrounded by spiders, or if he was on a stage in his underwear, and a spotlight was about to go on, exposing him to a packed audience? He wasn't normally afraid of the dark, but this was definitely creepy.

Then, in the darkness, he heard a faint noise. It was a whooshing sound, like the wind. Familiar, yet he couldn't quite place it. He felt something appear in his hand, something round and wooden. Just inches from his face, a giant flame appeared!

"Aah!" Alarmed, Holden dropped the flame to his feet. Floating above it, he saw a fading word: *torch*. Of course! That noise was the sound the words made when they came toward him. This was another part of the story being filled in. "Oh, thanks!" he said, bending down to pick up the torch. "Anything else?" He waited, but no other words came, so he figured he'd better get searching with the torch.

The light given off by the flame only illuminated a few feet in any direction, so Holden had to get a sense of his surroundings piece by piece. First, he held the torch in front of him and saw nothing but a wall of dirt.

Then, he turned around and saw that behind him was another wall of dirt.

He lowered the torch toward the ground. Dirt.

He raised it over his head. Dirt.

He was getting nowhere with this soft, flickering light. Then, he remembered he had the tablet in his coat, so he pulled it out and turned on his flashlight app.

Now everything was brightly illuminated, and Holden could clearly see that he was in a long, deep cave. "Ah, much better!" he said, gazing around him.

As Holden inspected the surroundings, he noticed a soft, shimmering light coming from his left, a golden glow reflecting back toward him. Since there wasn't anywhere else to go, he walked that way.

"Do you see it?" echoed a voice from above him.

Holden had no idea who was talking to him, but he figured the dude had to be referring to the golden glow. "Um, I think so," he said.

"Excellent!" said the voice.

Holden took one careful step after another toward the light, and soon, he saw where it was coming from. There, before his eyes, was a shiny golden . . . thing.

"Is it the lamp?" the voice from above asked.

Holden checked it over closely. "Nah, not really."

"No?" said the voice, confused.

"Well, it's not a regular lamp, like the one on my nightstand at home. I don't see a lightbulb or anything. I'd say it's more of a stretched-out teapot-looking doohickey."

"Are you trying to fool me?" said the voice, angrily.

"No. I mean, it's not what I would call a lamp, but I guess there's a chance it might light up or something."

"Quiet!" said the voice. "Bring it to me!"

As Holden stared at the object, he realized where he had seen it before. It was Aladdin's lamp, the one with the genie inside. He still wasn't sure exactly how this object could be considered a lamp, but lots of stuff was weird in fairy tales, so he figured he'd just go with it. If this was Aladdin's lamp, that could only mean one thing: Holden was totally Aladdin!

He gave the lamp a rub, then stood back and watched as a gray mist appeared through its nozzle. It stretched upward and expanded, taking the shape of a large, odd-looking man. The man had an extended jaw bone, a hunch in his back, and hair all over his body.

"Me genie," the hovering spirit grunted. "What want?"

Holden stared at the man strangely. "Of course! You're a Neanderthal!"

"Neander-what? I tell you. Me genie!" the genie said, annoyed. "Make three wish! What want?"

"Well, about those three wishes," Holden said. "I'm a little smarter than all the clowns you've had as a master until now. Things are going to go a little differently with me."

Before Holden could cast his wish for infinite wishes, the entire cave began to rumble. The walls shook violently, and dirt began to rain down from above.

"Whoa! What's going on?" Holden asked, covering his head with his hands and trying to keep from falling over.

The genie shrugged. "Cave roof fall down. You die soon."

Holden looked around frantically for an exit, but even with his tablet, he couldn't see one. He didn't know which way to run.

"Genie, help!" he shouted. "Fly me out of here!"

"As wish, Master!" the genie replied. He swept Holden up in his arms and flew him away. Together, they raced through the crumbling cave, dodging rivers of sand that quickly filled in the tunnel. There was only the narrowest of openings remaining. Holden closed his eyes as the genie aimed them right toward it.

Then, with a mighty whirl, the genie flew Holden out into the moonlit desert. Holden caught his breath, as the genie placed him gently down on a sand dune.

"Whoa, thanks, dude," Holden said. "You saved my life. Now, what was I saying?"

The genie bowed humbly before Holden. "You say other masters clowns. Now, two wish left."

"What do you mean? I didn't wish for anything!"

"You ask genie fly you out. That wish."

"Crud!" Holden shouted. He couldn't believe he had already wasted a wish, though if he had to do it, it did seem like not dying was a good wish to make.

"Okay, you got me," Holden admitted. "But you haven't outsmarted me, dude, because my second wish is going to be—"

"Hand me the lamp!" a cold, menacing voice shouted from behind Holden. It was the voice he had heard in the cave. Holden turned around and saw him, an evil-eyed sorcerer on horseback. He stared down his nose viciously at Holden. "It's mine! Mine!"

Holden rolled his eyes, unintimidated. "No way," he said. "Finders keepers, dude."

The sorcerer scowled and grumbled angrily, and he began to step down from his horse.

"Ooh, I'm really scared," Holden said sarcastically, but when he looked beside him, he noticed that the genie was quietly backing away. He looked terrified.

"Please . . . no hurt genie!" the genie whimpered.

Holden looked back at the sorcerer, suddenly afraid. "I said . . . ," the vile man continued, louder and more forcefully, "hand me the lamp . . . NOW!" He pulled a pointed scimitar from his side and rested its sharp blade against Holden's neck.

Holden gulped in terror. "Genie, help!" he said. "Make this dodo bird go away!"

"As wish!" the genie replied.

Instantly — POOF! — the evil sorcerer disappeared in a cloud of smoke, and when the smoke cleared, all that was left was a fluttering, crooked-beaked bird.

"Ah, a dodo bird!" Holden said. "I get it. Nice one!" No longer scary, the dodo bird flew away, and Holden breathed a sigh of relief.

"Thanks, man," Holden said. "I owe you."

"No, me owe you," the genie replied. "One wish more."

"Oh no you don't!" Holden replied. "You think you're so smart, but even if you count those as wishes, we're not done here. My third wish is for infinite wishes!" He stood back, hands on his hips, gloating.

The genie groaned. "Rats," he said. "You know loophole."

Chapter 6

Maddie cowered in the shadow of the mighty elephant as its foot came heaving down toward her.

"Wait!" Nazeerah shouted, spotting the helpless camel. The elephant looked down and saw it was about to crush the humped animal, so she swerved to the side at the last second.

Still, she couldn't help setting her massive foot down on Maddie's tail.

"Ouch!" Maddie shouted, as she yanked her tail free.

"Ouch?" Nazeerah repeated. She had never heard a camel say "ouch" before. Confused, she climbed down from the elephant's back and bent over the camel. "Did you say 'Ouch'?"

Maddie had to think fast. She tried her best to mimic the way the camels sounded. "Uh . . . bwuh-uh-uhhhh!" she brayed. The other camels all looked at her strangely, but it was enough to convince Nazeerah.

"You poor dear," the princess said, inspecting Maddie's injury. "You must come back to the palace with us, so we can tend to your tail."

Maddie smiled and nodded excitedly. "Bwuh-uh-uhh!"

Nazeerah shook her head, confused. "And your head, too. You don't seem quite right."

The guardsmen helped the princess climb back up onto her elephant, and they attached a harness to Maddie. Finally, she felt like she was making progress in this fairy tale.

Maddie remembered reading that camels were known for their endurance. They could travel hundreds of miles through the scorching desert heat without a single break to catch their breath or even a sip of water. Unfortunately, Maddie was just a girl in a camel's body. She could barely walk, let alone deal with these oppressive temperatures while lugging a huge hump across the desert. By the time Nazeerah's caravan arrived at the palace, she was pooped and craving a tall glass of lemonade.

She followed Nazeerah's elephant through the palace gates and was awed by the majesty of her surroundings. The palace towered over the desert, with ornate domes so tall they seemed to touch the stars in the sky. Musicians played gorgeous melodies while ladies danced and men charmed snakes. Exotic birds flitted freely to and fro through one lush courtyard after another. It was almost like being at the circus. They even passed by a huge bush that had been trimmed perfectly to resemble Nazeerah herself.

Maddie couldn't contain her excitement.

"Wow!" she gushed.

"Who said 'wow'?" Nazeerah asked, peering down from the elephant's back. "You've all seen my palace a thousand times. There's never anything new around here." She sighed deeply. Maddie couldn't believe someone who lived in such an amazing place could seem so bored.

It's then that Maddie heard the sound of water splashing. She spotted an ornate fountain several stories high and rushed over to it, licking her lips. As soon as she got there, she plunged her entire head into the water, lapping it up with her massive, flip-flopping tongue.

A man appeared on the palace steps. "At last, my daughter has returned!" he boomed, arms outstretched to welcome her home. The Sultan wore a long white robe and a jewel-encrusted turban. He was very happy to see his daughter.

"Hello, Father!" Nazeerah responded, climbing down and giving her father a hug.

The Sultan looked at all the packages being unloaded from Nazeerah's caravan. "My, what a lot of things you've picked up at the bazaar. Is this all for the wedding?"

"Yes, Father," Nazeerah said. "I was thinking we could invite everyone. The whole kingdom!"

"Well, that's a big decision," the Sultan said. "Are you sure that's best?"

"Yes, I think so," Nazeerah replied, a little hesitant.

"Better ask Prince Haroun what he thinks," the Sultan said. "He is going to be the next sultan, after all."

The Sultan bid his daughter farewell and returned to the palace. Nazeerah kicked sand with her foot, glumly, as another man arrived to greet her.

"My dear, sweet, beautiful bride!" he called out, waltzing into the courtyard. He was buff and handsome. He wore the finest silk thobe and stood with the straightest posture Maddie had ever seen. But Nazeerah could not have been more depressed at the sight of him.

"Hello, Haroun," she replied, as he kissed the back of her hand.

"My goodness!" Haroun said, gazing around at all the goods Nazeerah brought back with her from the bazaar. "Is all of this for our wedding?"

"Yes," Nazeerah explained. "I love my royal subjects so much, I was thinking we could invite everyone to join in our celebration."

Haroun laughed. "Don't be silly!" he said. "The royal wedding is a special occasion. We can't just let in all the riff-raff off the street."

"But we have so much, and so many in this kingdom go without," Nazeerah pleaded.

Haroun tutted. "If they're not happy with what they've been given in life, they should work harder to find a genie."

Maddie was disgusted by his attitude. She was hoping Nazeerah would stand up to him, but instead, the princess just lowered her head and backed away. Maddie wished more than ever that she had come into this story as Nazeerah rather than a camel. Then, she could tell this guy exactly what a creep he was and be rid of him. Clearly, Nazeerah didn't have the courage to do so herself.

"Now go rest," Haroun said. "Let me handle all the preparations. All you need to worry about is your dress."

"But—"

Haroun cut her off. "Servants, dispose of this waste!" He clapped his hands, and all the servants sprang into action, carting away the goods Nazeerah had purchased at the bazaar. Then, just as quickly, Haroun was gone, leaving Nazeerah alone and sulking in the courtyard.

Maddie felt horrible for her. She hated to see such a kind woman treated like a child. Of course, this was exactly how the story was supposed to go. Nazeerah was unhappy with her fiancé. Now, she would meet Aladdin and choose to marry him instead. Even a camel could keep this story on track.

So why did Maddie feel so uneasy?

Chapter
7

"Must tell you," the genie said. "One thing no can wish for."
He and Holden were standing by the ruins of the mystical
cave, in an otherwise empty stretch of desert.

"It's not a hoverboard is it?" Holden said.

"No. Is love."

"Yuck!" Holden blurted out, laughing. "As if!"

"What? Every master ever want love," the genie said,
stunned. "You no want girlfriend?"

"Gross!" Holden said. "I don't need a girlfriend. I need
a hoverboard!"

"A hover-huh?" the genie asked.

"Board!" Holden rolled his eyes. "A hover*board*. It's like
a flying carpet, but smaller and cooler."

"Smaller, cooler. Yes, can do!" the genie said. He waved
his hands and — POOF! A tiny object appeared in front
of him. It was only an inch big, and it had icicles dripping
from it.

"What is that?" Holden asked. He leaned in for a closer look and saw that the object was a carpet that had been frozen solid.

"Is smaller, cooler flying carpet," the genie replied. "Ha ha ha!"

"Hilarious," Holden responded, swatting the carpet away. "I see how you operate. You take everything I say literally. I called that guy a dodo bird, so you made him a dodo bird. I asked for a cool carpet, so you gave me a frozen one. Very clever. That's probably supposed to make me regret what I wished for, so I realize I was better off before I had a genie in the first place. Right?"

"How you know so much about genies?" The genie looked Holden up and down, skeptically. "You rotten kid cursed by Resplenda?"

"Oh, you know Resplenda? Well, I don't care what she told you. I'm not rotten. I'm just honest," Holden replied.

The genie groaned. "Uggggh!" He gazed around him, as if talking to an unseen person. "You right, Resplenda. He verrrrry rotten."

"Well, like it or not, you're my genie now," Holden said. "You have to do what I say, and I don't want you teaching me any lessons, so I'm going to be specific. Now, can I please have an iJet ZX-4500 Ultra Hoverjammer from Sizzletech Industries of Sandusky, Ohio. In black and hot pink. With a skull on it. The standard size and temperature."

"Boo!" the genie jeered. "Me want yawn." He waved his hands and — POOF! He conjured exactly the hoverboard Holden had always wanted. "Boring!"

"Sweet!" Holden said. He climbed onto the hoverboard, and it began to float above the desert. As soon as he leaned forward, he and the board zoomed toward the horizon.

"Whoooooooaaaa!" Holden shouted, kicking up a huge cloud of sand as he roared across the landscape. He swayed and flipped, then turned around and rocketed back toward the genie. It was the greatest rush of his life. He was going so fast he could feel himself starting to sweat. He even saw smoke rising from his feet. He was burning up this desert!

No, wait. Why was there smoke? He looked down at his feet and saw that his hoverboard was on fire!

"Aaaaaaah!" Holden screamed, leaping into a sand dune for safety. The board crashed to the ground a few feet away, engulfed in flames. "Wow," Holden said, watching it burn. "I guess my mom was right."

"Should have stuck with cool one!" the genie laughed.

"Okay, let's try that again. I want the same hoverboard, but fireproof."

The genie waved his hands. POOF! The flaming wreck disappeared, and a shiny new hoverboard appeared in its place.

"Yes!" Holden cheered. "Now conjure me the biggest, sickest skate park in the whole desert!"

POOF! Another tiny object appeared in front of Holden. He reached out and grabbed it, pulling it in for a closer look.

It was a miniature skate park, barely big enough for an ant to skateboard on.

"I said I wanted the biggest one!"

"How many skate park you think desert have?" the genie replied. "That the biggest."

The miniature skate park began to shake. It made a sound as if it were inhaling uncomfortably. "Ah . . . ah . . ."

"What's it doing now?" Holden asked.

"What you ask for," the genie said.

"CHOO!!!!" exhaled the skate park, sneezing a massive spray of snot all over Holden.

"You want it sick. Ha ha ha!" The genie laughed at his own joke, while Holden wiped the snot from his face.

"You're not going to make this easy, are you?" Holden said.

Genie smirked. "No way! That no fun!"

Chapter 8

As badly as Maddie wanted to help Nazeerah, she spent most of the afternoon with her head shoved in the fountain, drinking as much as her pink, wormy tongue could lap up. She knew camels could store enough in their humps that they could go weeks on end without drinking, but she must have inhabited this camel's body when its hump was running on empty. No amount of water seemed to satisfy her intense thirst. Finally, a guard came across her and chased her away. "Get out of there, filthy camel!" he shouted. "Disgusting!"

Maddie was actually grateful to get away from the fountain. It was distracting her from what really mattered: getting Nazeerah to meet Aladdin so that they could fall in love. Still, despite all the water she'd taken in, all she could think about was finding more. In one of the gardens, she heard the sound of a bubbling brook, and she began walking toward it as if by instinct. *I'll just take a few sips*, she thought to herself, *and then I'll save Nazeerah.*

When she reached the brook, she cringed at what she saw. The water was murky and foul, filled with slimy rocks and dead bugs. It was about the least appealing thing she could imagine drinking, but before she knew it — splash! She plunged her head in the water and began lapping it up.

"PFFFFFFT!" Maddie backed away from the brook and spat out everything in her mouth. Apparently, even camels had standards. It wasn't the bugs or the dirt that bothered her, though. It was something else. The water tasted sour. Soapy.

Then she heard the sound of women laughing and talking softly. She gazed upstream and saw some of the maidens of the palace doing laundry. Furious, she began stomping angrily toward them. How dare they wash their clothes in the water she was drinking! She had the strong urge to kick sand in their faces.

Before she reached them, though, she heard some of the things they were saying.

"It's amazing. A palace sprung up in the desert overnight!"

"They say he's wealthy and handsome and makes magic!"

Maddie's ears perked up. They were talking about Aladdin! She casually walked just upstream from them and eavesdropped.

"How could one man build a palace for himself overnight?" one woman asked.

Another woman motioned for them all to lean in so she could share a secret. "I heard," she whispered, "that he found a genie!"

The other women gasped.

"You know who's not going to like that someone else has built a palace in the kingdom?"

The women all shuddered and said in unison, "Prince Haroun." Clearly, they weren't any fonder of this guy than Nazeerah was. Maddie wished she could join in their conversation, but camels weren't supposed to talk. They were supposed to drink water, and that's all Maddie could seem to do.

"You can stop washing the tablecloths," a voice called out. The women looked over and were stunned to see Princess Nazeerah approaching. They instantly stopped what they were doing and bowed down to her.

"Your Highness!" they said.

"The wedding will be much smaller than I had hoped," Nazeerah continued.

"I thought you were inviting the entire kingdom," one of the women said.

"No, that plan has changed," Nazeerah replied, hanging her head. "Prince Haroun wants royalty only."

The women glanced at each other knowingly. Maddie was hoping one of them would speak up and tell Nazeerah what they really thought of Haroun, but they were all too nervous.

"If that's what His Highness wants," one said.

"Yes," Nazeerah sighed. "He was quite clear about it."

The women nodded softly. Maddie was disappointed. She thought Nazeerah's servants would look out for her. Were they really going to let their beloved princess marry this horrible man without speaking up? Well, if they weren't going to say something, Maddie would.

"Do you love him?" Maddie asked, forgetting momentarily that she was a camel.

Nazeerah turned back toward the women, thinking it had been one of them who posed the question.

"Who said that?"

The women all looked at each other, uncomfortably. One of them meekly pointed toward Maddie. "I think it was the camel," she said softly.

"It's all right," Nazeerah replied. "You don't have to tell me. Whoever it was, I appreciate your honesty. The truth is I don't know. How can you know what love is until you've felt it? I've only read about it in books. I just wish Prince Haroun wouldn't treat me like such a . . . a . . . princess!"

Nazeerah turned around to leave again. Feeling bold, Maddie spoke up once more. "Maybe you should meet this Aladdin guy. He'd be a lot better for you."

This time, all the women except Nazeerah saw who had spoken. They turned quizzically toward the camel, wondering if their eyes were deceiving them.

"The man with the palace in the desert?" Nazeerah said, looking back toward the women. She was the only one who didn't realize now that it was the camel who was talking. "He does sound interesting, doesn't he? I'm so curious to know what he's like."

Nazeerah smiled, staring longingly into space, then she shook herself out of it, and her frown returned. "But how would I get there? I can't take the royal caravan, or Prince

Haroun will know where I'm headed." Nazeerah walked back toward the palace.

All the women turned toward Maddie now, wondering what to do. Maddie no longer saw the point in pretending to be an ordinary camel. "Just take this camel," she said.

Nazeerah turned back toward the women, smiling. "You know what?" she said. "I think that might actually work. Okay, I'll do it! Will you please saddle her up while I get my coat?" She jogged inside, and the women all turned toward Maddie, amazed at what this camel had just orchestrated.

"You heard her," Maddie said to the perplexed women. "Saddle me up!"

Chapter
9

"Let's see," Nazeerah wondered aloud. "They say his palace sprung up suddenly in the North, so we should follow the North Star." She pulled on Maddie's reins to steer her in that direction, and Maddie changed course with ease. She was really starting to get the hang of walking like a camel now. She could even do it with a passenger on her back.

Maddie looked up at the sky to make note of where the North Star was, marveling at how clear and beautiful night in the desert was. The air was soft and pure. The golden moon cast a hazy, orange glow over the sand that made it feel magical and alive. The stars were absolutely brilliant, from the bright white constellations to the sprays of green and purple shooting across the sky.

Wait a second. Green and purple? Those weren't stars. Those were fireworks. Maddie listened closely to the sound of them popping and crackling in the distance. Nazeerah noticed them, too.

"What are those amazing lights?" she asked.

Maddie wasn't sure if fireworks existed in Arabia. They had to be coming from Aladdin's palace. Well, that would definitely make finding him much easier.

Maddie followed the fireworks as they spread across the sky in incredible patterns. Some of them burst out in red, white, and blue, just like the ones her family saw on the Fourth of July. *That's odd,* Maddie thought. Those are American colors, not Arabian. Why would Aladdin choose those colors? Then, she got a better indication of why the fireworks seemed so familiar.

"What does that say?" Nazeerah wondered aloud. She squinted her eyes at the latest display of lights above them. They seemed to spell out words. "Al . . . ?" Nazeerah read, as she tried to make out the rest of the words.

Maddie could see them very well, though, and to her, the words were perfectly clear: *ALADDIN RULZ.*

Maddie rolled her eyes. She should've guessed it. Holden was Aladdin!

No wonder she hadn't seen him yet. He was too busy enjoying his unlimited wishes to come find Nazeerah. Well, at least now she knew what she had to do to fix this fairy tale: she had to get Nazeerah to fall in love with her stepbrother.

Yikes, poor Nazeerah, she thought. The princess had to fall in love with a guy who saved his old scabs in a jar on the bathroom sink? Who once wore the same *Star Wars* T-shirt five days in a row? Whose favorite form of entertainment was watching videos of people falling down stairs? This certainly wasn't going to be easy.

The fireworks led Maddie and Nazeerah toward a magnificent castle. As they got closer, the explosions rattled out with the speed and volume of a machine gun. POP! POP! POP! They were so loud, Nazeerah had to cover her ears.

"You're a brave one!" Nazeerah said, petting Maddie's head. "Most camels run away from loud noises."

Maddie smiled and replied, "Well, I just really think you should meet this guy."

She thought Nazeerah would appreciate her honesty. Maybe she'd even be convinced to give Aladdin a try. Maddie wasn't expecting the way Nazeerah actually reacted.

"AAAAAH! A talking camel!" Nazeerah screeched in horror. She pushed herself backward across the desert, drawing away from Maddie as fast as she could.

Maddie had totally forgotten for a moment that she was an animal. "Oh, sorry," Maddie said. "You weren't supposed to hear that. I mean, I wasn't supposed to say anything. I mean, hey, I'm a *good* talking camel!"

"AAAAAH!" Nazeerah sprinted away from Maddie across the desert.

Great, Maddie thought. *Now what?*

Holden figured it would probably be a good idea if he started looking for Maddie in this fairy tale sometime soon. Unfortunately, he had this thought while tricking off a halfpipe against the backdrop of the super sweet palace he owned. So he quickly put it out of his mind and went back to thinking about how this was the most awesome fairy tale ever.

He had everything he had ever wanted — his own skate park, a giant tank of man-eating sharks, a laser tag arena full of karate-chopping robot opponents. He gazed out upon it all while doing a 360 in the air on his hoverboard a hundred feet high. He kept spinning until it became a 720, then a 1080! He did another full revolution, but he couldn't do the math in his head to figure out what to call it, so he decided to stop there and return to the ground.

"Wow!" he heard a woman say, as he set down. "That was incredible!"

Holden hovered over to her, shrugging and doing his best to play it cool. "Eh, I could've kept going," he said, "but I didn't want to show off."

He looked at Nazeerah, who seemed to have staggered up to him out of the desert. She was beautiful and dressed in elegant clothes, like some kind of princess or something. He suddenly became very suspicious. "Wait a second. Who are you?"

She smiled coyly, since everyone in the kingdom knew who she was. "Don't you know?"

Holden groaned. Of course. This had to be Maddie. He knew she'd show up sooner or later to ruin his fun. "Yeah, I know who you are. And I'm Aladdin. Fine, you found me."

Nazeerah was confused. "Found you?"

"Look, I'm having too much fun to deal with you right this second. Why don't you hit the buffet for a few while I take a dip in the whirlpool?" He hopped back on his hoverboard and scooted away.

Nazeerah was taken aback by this man's brash behavior. She had never met anyone before who didn't bow down and flatter her instantly. It was . . . it was kind of refreshing, actually. After the long camel ride through the desert, she was quite hungry, so she decided to do as this man suggested and look at the buffet table. She found it full of strange and exotic foods. Chicken in tiny nugget shapes. Slices of bread with fruit preserves and a brown spread that tasted like peanuts. Most unusual of all were some long sticks wrapped in crunchy brown crumbs. When she bit into one, gooey cheese melted out. Mmm-mmm! They were delicious. She soon discovered these delicacies tasted even better when dipped in a red tomato sauce.

Maddie peered out from behind a bush to see what Nazeerah was doing. She was very careful not to let the princess see her again, for fear of alarming her further. It was bad enough that Holden had abandoned Nazeerah when he was supposed to be romancing her. Maybe he needed a talking camel to set him straight.

There was no longer any doubt in Maddie's mind that this palace was wished into existence by her nutty stepbrother. There were LCD screens three stories high showing extreme sports like BMX and snowboarding. Massive fountains spouted what appeared to be energy drinks. Instead of staircases, there were trampolines people used to bounce from one floor to another. The entire structure shook with the sound of loud rock music. It took Maddie a minute to realize that the noise wasn't coming from an MP3 player. Holden's favorite band, Hashtag Number Sign, was rocking out on a stage — live!

It was Holden's dream come true — and Maddie's worst nightmare. She looked all over the property for Holden, past the looping slides and wave pool of what had to be the only water park in the desert. Then, she saw something strange and glowing hovering off the ground. It was a man, a man who seemed to be made from mist, halfway between a human and a ghost. He was huge and hairy, with terrible posture. She remembered what Holden said about how the genie would be a Neanderthal, and she realized that's who this must be.

"I'm not crazy about this swimsuit," Holden was saying to the genie. "Could you conjure me a new one? Blue . . . no, bright red. No . . . tell you what, just conjure every swimsuit in the world ever, and I'll pick one."

"As wish," the genie said, sounding weary and annoyed.

Maddie strode up to Holden, ready to set him straight.

Before she could open her mouth, though, Holden spotted her coming. "Another thing," he said to the genie. "I'm sick of all these camels everywhere. Can you have them all get hit with meteors?"

"Holden, wait!" Maddie shouted. "Don't do it!"

Holden stood up in shock. "A talking camel? I never wished for that!"

"Holden, it's me!"

Holden took a good look at the animal. It was a camel, all right, but there was something familiar about it, something in the shape of its face that was somewhat human. The more he stared at it, the clearer it became. "Maddie? You're a camel?" he guffawed. "This fairy tale just gets better and better!"

Now Maddie was really angry. "Is this why you wished us into this fairy tale? So you could get a hoverboard, and I could be a camel?"

Holden shook his head. "I had no idea you'd be a camel. That was just a sweet bonus. So does that mean that nagging princess was really—"

"The real Princess Nazeerah, who you're supposed to fall in love with."

"Oops," Holden said. "I guess I was kind of a creep to her."

"Holden!"

"It was only because I thought she was you!" Holden shrugged. "Well, I guess we'll be stuck in this story a while longer. Do camels swim? Hop in. The water's great!" He reclined in his pool, relaxing, no longer concerned about the story.

"Holden, we need to fix this fairy tale, and there's very little I can do as a camel. I tried to talk to Princess Nazeerah, and she nearly had a stroke!"

"Whoa, that sounds funny. I wonder if any of my security cameras caught it."

"Enough, Holden. Change me now!"

"Oh, fine," he said. "Genie, forget the swimsuit thing. Come here." Holden whispered in the genie's ear.

"As wish," Genie said, and he began to wave his arms.

"Thank you," Maddie said. "I'm sure camels are wonderful animals, but I was getting a little tired of all the cud-chewing."

As the genie worked his magic, Maddie rose up in a cloud of sparkling dust. Holden watched in awe as she swirled around and then set back down on the ground . . .

"Thank you, Holden. Now we can finally get you and the princess together. Now, where did she go?" Maddie looked around, then decided she needed a higher vantage point.

She leapt up several feet above her toward a water slide. She gripped it with her long brown tail and swung upside-down to search for Nazeerah. It was only as she was scanning the area that she realized she didn't normally choose to hang upside-down like this. Nor did she have a long brown tail, for that matter.

She caught her reflection in the pool below. She wasn't a camel anymore, but she wasn't a human either.

"Holden!" she shouted, examining her furry new body. "You made me a monkey?"

"HAHAHAHAHAHA!" he cackled. "Well, you said you didn't want to be a camel anymore."

"How am I supposed to do anything as a monkey?"

"I don't know, but here comes the princess," Holden said. "You'd better stay quiet. I hear she doesn't like talking animals. Genie, maybe you should beat it, too."

"As wish, Master," the genie said, and he joined Maddie at the top of the waterslide, where the two of them watched

Princess Nazeerah approaching Holden, chewing on another cheese stick.

"Where did you find all this strange and exotic food?" she asked.

"It's just a mozzarella stick," Holden shrugged.

"It's the most delicious thing I've ever tasted."

"Yeah, they're pretty great, but have you ever tried a jalapeño popper?"

"A what?" Princess Nazeerah asked.

"Here," Holden said, tossing her a deep-fried pepper. "Enjoy."

Princess Nazeerah chewed on the treat, her face breaking out into a huge smile . . . that quickly turned into a shocked gasp. "It's so . . . hot!" she said.

"Here, quick," Holden said. "Wash it down with some Ten Hours of Power Juice."

He stuck a cup under one of his fountains and caught some energy drink in it, then handed it to Nazeerah. "Mmm!" she said, as she gulped it down. "This is the most wonderful cuisine I've ever had!"

"No duh," Holden said. "I mean, falafel's okay, but I can't imagine eating it 24/7."

"Your palace is amazing," Nazeerah informed him, gazing around at the immense structure the genie had conjured for Holden. "My father would never let me have all these strange and dangerous things."

"Yeah, parents are the worst, aren't they?" Holden said.

"You mustn't speak that way of the Sultan!" Princess Nazeerah gasped.

"Hey, you said it, not me." He rose from his hot tub and held out his hand. "I'm Hold— uh, Aladdin."

"Aladdin," Nazeerah smiled. "I've heard about you. Can I ask what that magical device you were riding on was?"

"The hoverboard? I thought all girls hated them."

"Hate?! No! It's wonderful!" Nazeerah said. "Do you think I could have a ride?"

"You're sure your dad wouldn't mind?" Holden replied.

"I'm sure he would! That's why I want to do it!"

Holden nodded, impressed. Nazeerah wasn't like any girl he went to school with, that was for sure. Those girls always thought he was weird or annoying. Nazeerah was surprisingly cool. He had spent five seconds talking to her and didn't want to run away, puking his guts out. That was a new record for him.

Besides, Maddie was on his case trying to get him to hang out with Nazeerah, so he might as well get it over with. He grabbed his hoverboard, but then he stopped himself. "Hmmm . . . I know something else we could ride. Something that would really blow your dad's mind."

Holden stepped away and whispered for the genie. "Psst, Genie! I need a bigger hoverboard. Something that can fit me and the princess together. But it has to be aerodynamic so it can go fast and do cool tricks."

"As wish," the Genie said. He waved his hands, and a flying carpet appeared.

Holden shrugged. "Yeah, that'll work."

The genie shook his head and walked away, annoyed. "Not easy being his master," he said as he passed by Maddie.

"Try being his stepsister," Maddie replied.

Chapter 10

"So it's true what they say?" Nazeera asked, as Holden helped her onto a carpet that hovered two feet over the sand. "You found a genie?"

"Found him?" Holden bragged. "I saved him! Poor dude was trapped in a lamp. He was so grateful, he does everything I ask."

"That's so nice," Nazeerah said. "What's his name?"

"I call him Genie," Holden replied. "I think that's his name."

The carpet rose up toward the sky, higher than Nazeerah could've imagined. "Whoa!" she exclaimed, as she got a glimpse of the desert. Sand dunes sprawled out in every direction, flecked occasionally by the lights of villages. "I've never seen the kingdom from this height. It's positively—"

"Not as lame?" Holden cracked.

"You think the desert is lame?" she said.

"It's okay, if you like sand," Holden replied. "Where I come from, we have forests and mountains. There's even this place called the Grand Canyon. I mean, that's just a bunch of dirt, too, but at least they did something cool with it."

"I've never been outside the desert," Nazeerah said. "I only wish I could see the kinds of places you talk about."

"Did you say wish?" Holden smiled. "Well, check this out! Hey, Genie!"

"As wish!" echoed a sound from below, and in an instant, the magic carpet took off like a shot, zooming over the desert at breathtaking speed. "Oh, my!" Nazeera shouted. "This is not how a member of royalty usually travels," Nazeerah said, breathless.

"Eh, get over yourself, Princess!" Holden responded.

"Get over myself?" she repeated.

"Yeah, you're full of the same goop and guts as me or anyone else, so if you're enjoying this, just enjoy it. What's the big deal?"

"You're right," Nazeerah smiled. "Take me somewhere wonderful!"

"You bet!" Holden winked, and the carpet sped up again, heading for the horizon.

Soon, the carpet soared over a lush, dense jungle. There was color everywhere, splashes of green, red, and orange.

"I never knew this existed!" Princess Nazeerah said.

"You're awfully sheltered for a princess," Holden replied. "Good thing you met me, huh?"

They whizzed past baboons swinging from vines and snakes slithering up the trunks of trees. They rode through flashes of rain and patches of brilliant sunlight. They swooped down to the ground then soared way up high above it all.

Soon, they found themselves gliding across an African savannah. They dipped down toward a pack of gazelles and gaped at miles and miles of untamed brush teeming with exotic wildlife. Next, they were crossing the ocean, and Holden hovered low enough to splash the princess playfully. She gasped as she saw dolphins leaping out of the water, seeming to wave hello to them with their fins.

Princess Nazeerah was having the time of her life.

Maddie was sure Holden was blowing it, big time.

In her experience, girls simply didn't like her stepbrother. He was obnoxious, loud, sarcastic, and impossible to please. He was everything that girls didn't like about boys, all wrapped up in one boyish body. And he was their only ticket home. Somehow, someway, they needed to get Princess Nazeerah to fall head over heels for him.

"We're doomed," Maddie moaned, turning to the genie. "So what's it like being stuck somewhere for a gazillion years, Genie?"

Genie sighed. "Well, Monkey, it stink."

"Oh no," Maddie explained. "A monkey is what I am, but it's not my name. My name is Maddie."

"Well, genie what I am, but it not my name."

"It's not?" Maddie asked. "Then what is your name?"

"It Geeno."

"Geeno?" Maddie repeated. "That sounds like Genie."

"Well, Monkey sound like Maddie!" he said, grunting angrily.

"I guess you're right."

"Yes, I right!" Geeno replied. Annoyed, he crossed his arms and turned his back to her.

"I'm sorry," Maddie said. "I didn't mean to hurt your feelings."

"Geeno very sensitive about being genie," Geeno explained.

"Well, I don't want to be a monkey any more than you want to be a genie, so maybe we can work together."

Geeno turned around, still pouting. "I listening," he said.

"Okay, we need to get the princess to fall in love with your master and my stepbrother."

Genie sighed. "In that case, I be genie forever."

"Hold on," Maddie said. "I think I have an idea."

Holden and Nazeerah hovered over the South Pole, watching penguins sliding down glaciers and splashing into the chilly waters of the Antarctic.

"They're so adorable! I never knew a place like this existed. It's so cold and beautiful! What's next?" Nazeerah said.

"Eh, that's about it," Holden shrugged.

"Really?"

"Yeah. Mountains, jungles, forests, the Antarctic. Everyplace else is pretty lame."

"Oh," Nazeerah said. An awkward silence passed between them.

Just then, a strange bird flew past the magic carpet. It flitted up close to Holden's ear. "*Psst!*" it whispered. "*Psst!*"

Holden couldn't think of any birds that were known to make a "*Psst!*" sound, and when he looked over he figured out why. It had the body and wings of a bird, but its face was that of his genie.

"Is that you?" Holden said, covering his mouth so Nazeerah wouldn't hear.

"Yeah, you boring her!"

"So?" Holden shrugged, completely unconcerned.

"You sister say be romantic."

"No way! I'm not saying a bunch of corny, lovey nonsense."

"Ugh, foolish boy!" Genie groaned. "No have talk. Just sing!"

"Sing? Well, I can do that! Dude, I totally rock!"

"No, sing romantic song!"

"Romantic? I don't know any cheesy romantic songs."

"Think!" Genie demanded.

Holden tried to think hard. Hashtag Number Sign did a song about how much fun it would be to turn into zombies with someone and then eat each other's brains. Was that romantic? Probably not. More likely, the genie wanted Holden to sing Princess Nazeerah a song like that sappy ballad his mom and Greg danced to at their wedding. The one where the guy talks about all the beautiful things he sees when he looks in some lady's eyes.

It was pretty much the nuttiest song Holden had ever heard. Whenever he looked in someone's eyes, all he saw were disgusting things like veins and eye boogers. He was going to have to fake this.

"Hmmmmm," he hummed. That got Nazeerah's attention. She smiled at him, so she seemed to be into the whole song thing. Now he just had to think of some words to fill in the melody. "In your eyes, I see . . . rainbows. And flower buds and puppy toes!" He didn't love it, but at least it rhymed. And Nazeerah was still smiling a little bit, so he figured he'd keep going.

"I see key lime pie and stars in the sky. There's nothing gross at all in your eyes!"

Nazeerah could hardly stand to listen to Holden's off-key singing, but she didn't want to hurt his feelings, so she did her best to continue smiling.

Holden, seeing the look on her face, figured he was nailing it. He decided to go for a high note.

"In your EYEEEEEEEES!"

Nazeerah may have been able to fake her politeness, but all around them, the birds weren't quite so kind. They began to squawk loudly over Holden's shrieking voice. Holden assumed that if even the animals were responding to his song, he must be really awesome. What he didn't know was that they thought one of their flock was injured, so they were making a distress call. Soon, birds from all over the area were circling the magic carpet to make sure everything was okay.

Chapter 11

When the Genie returned to Maddie, she was devouring an apple, spraying little bits of fruit everywhere. "So?" she said, spitting applesauce in every direction. "How did it go?"

The genie smiled proudly and transformed back into his old body. "It work. Probably they play smoochyface now!"

As he said these words, the carpet flew overhead, silhouetted against the moon. Maddie marveled at how romantic the sight was. She wished someday a guy might take her on a cruise around the globe on a clear, starry night. Surely, Nazeerah was swooning by now. Even Holden wouldn't be able to mess this up.

Then Maddie saw the flock of birds surrounding the carpet, sending out their distress call. From amid the ruckus, she heard an even worse sound: Holden's singing voice. She had forgotten how horrible it was. It was so bad that no one ever had the heart to tell him how bad it was. Instead, they would say things that sounded like compliments but really weren't. Things like, "That was . . . unique" and "I've never heard singing like that before."

"There's more great things in your eyes than I would ever think," Holden wailed, taking a deep breath for his big finish. "So I hope you keep them open and never ever bliiiiiiiiiiiink!"

Holden was so wrapped up in his song now that he didn't notice Nazeerah was covering her ears. As the carpet came to a stop at his palace, Holden dropped to his knees and let rip a monster air guitar solo. "Neer-neer-neer-neeeeeeeeeer!" he wailed, trying to mimic the sound of an electric guitar. It was even more eardrum-shattering than his singing. Maddie groaned. She had heard him do this in his bedroom many times while listening to his awful music.

"That was . . . unique," Nazeerah commented, when Holden finally quieted down.

"Yeah, I get that a lot," Holden bragged. "I'll bet you've never heard singing like that before."

Nazeerah shook her head uncomfortably. "No, I haven't."

"Well, let me sing you another song. Ever heard 'Zombie Brain Buffet' by Hashtag Number Sign? Hey, Genie! Can I get a microphone and a speaker a hundred feet high?"

Nazeerah stepped off the carpet and nervously backed away. "It's so late. I should go home before my father realizes I'm gone."

"No prob," Holden said. "I'll video it for you." He began to walk away, strumming an air guitar. "Later!"

Nazeerah stood uncomfortably, in the shadow of his giant water park, wondering how she would get home now.

Maddie scampered up to Holden, climbing him like a tree. She perched on his shoulder so she could speak directly into his ear. "You goon!" she said. "You have to make sure your date gets home safely. She's stuck in a desert!"

"Fine, fine," Holden said. "Genie! I wish for Nazeerah to get home safely."

"As wish," Geeno said. He waved his arms and summoned the magic carpet for Nazeerah. "This take you palace," he told her.

Maddie rapped Holden on the arm. "Don't let her go!"

"But you said to make sure she gets home safely!"

"Yes," Maddie replied, "but first you have to make plans to see her again, so she'll know you're interested."

Holden sighed. "This is why I'm never going to date, ever!" He ran up to the carpet, tapping Nazeerah on the shoulder. "Hang on a sec," he said. "So, like, you busy tomorrow?"

"Kind of. I'm getting married."

"Oh, right. Bummer."

"Yes," Nazeerah agreed. "Bummer."

"Well, aren't you supposed to be happy about it? Most girls get so gushy and annoying when they talk about their wedding day."

"I used to dream of my wedding day. I had visions of a grand celebration, a fabulous dress, and a man so charming he made my heart beat faster. This is just not how I pictured it."

"So cancel it," Holden said.

"Cancel the wedding?"

"Yeah, it'll be a big scandal. People will run around slamming doors and breaking dishes. Everyone will talk about you. It'll be so cool."

Nazeerah laughed. "I'm afraid I can't. I have to do as my father wishes, and he wants me to marry a prince."

"Man, your dad sounds even worse than my mom. Why can't parents just let us do what we want?"

"I don't understand his rules sometimes," Nazeerah said, "but I cannot disobey him. Well, I should go."

"See ya," Holden said, waving. He hopped back on the magic carpet and flew away. When he turned around, he was stunned to see Maddie glaring at him angrily. "What? Did I mess something else up?"

"Holden, you can fix this all right now if you'll just wish to become a prince. Then Nazeerah can marry you, and we can go home."

"No way!" Holden protested. "That's my whole point about this story. Aladdin shouldn't have to change who he is to get some girl to marry him. If that means we can't go home, I'll just have to stay here forever and play *Splatter Battalion 6*."

"Holden! You're not allowed to play that game!"

Holden smirked. "I'm allowed to do whatever I want here." He hopped on his hoverboard and went whizzing through the front door of his palace.

The genie hovered up to Maddie. "He stink."

Maddie nodded. "We'll never get home. He loves it here, because he doesn't have to listen to our parents."

"Hmm," Geeno said, deep in thought. "Understand. Geeno have parents, too."

"You did? So you were a regular guy?"

"Oh yes," Geeno said. "I hunter."

"A hunter? Really?"

"Yes," Geeno replied. "Best hunter in tribe. I so good, people do everything Geeno need. Have servant who make Geeno clothes and another who wash Geeno clothes. Have one servant pick Geeno nose and another eat it. One day, Geeno find woman with hand stuck under rock. She ask help. But I alone. So I go home and send servant help woman."

"Let me guess," Maddie said. "That woman ended up being a really weird fairy named Resplenda? And she cursed you to be other people's servant to teach you a lesson?"

"Right, she curse you, too, huh?"

"Yeah."

"Wow, she stink."

"So what do you have to do to break your spell?"

"Must get master wish for Geeno freedom."

"Well, I'll tell you what," Maddie said. "If you can help me, I'll get Holden to wish for your freedom."

"Him? Never work. How Geeno convince him give up unlimited wishes?"

"Well, he just wants to do things our parents won't let him do. Maybe you can use that to convince him to go to the wedding banquet. Meanwhile, I'll see if I can get him on the guest list."

"How you do that?"

"I'm a monkey," Maddie said. "I'll have to do some monkey business."

Chapter 12

Reaching Nazeerah's palace on tiny monkey legs took a lot longer than Maddie expected. She only wished she could've made the trip on a magic carpet. By the time she reached her destination, she was wiped out and even thirstier than she'd been as a camel. Thankfully, she knew just where the fountain was this time. She climbed up the palace wall, using her claw-like hands and tail to maintain her hold and balance.

Being a monkey, she decided, was much better than being a camel.

Before she reached the fountain, though, she was stopped by the sound of a woman weeping. "Father, it's not fair!" she said.

It was Nazeerah! Maddie abandoned her quest for water and followed the crying sound toward the princess.

"I'm sorry, dear," the Sultan replied. "But Prince Haroun was quite clear about the guest list. His family will be traveling here from far across the kingdom, and he doesn't want them mixing with what he called riff-raff."

"They're not riff-raff! They're our royal subjects, and I care about them!" Maddie loved hearing Nazeerah stand up for herself. If there was one thing she didn't like about fairy tales, it was their old-fashioned views about what girls could and couldn't do. So many princesses just sat around waiting for a prince to rescue them — lame! This was Nazeerah's wedding, too, after all. Shouldn't she be able to choose whom to invite? And more importantly, shouldn't she be able to choose whom to marry? Prince Haroun wasn't Nazeerah's type at all.

"Nazeerah!" the Sultan said sternly. "Prince Haroun will be your husband, and he will be our sultan. You need to get used to him making the decisions."

Maddie continued climbing toward the window. She could feel that Nazeerah was about to let loose on her dad, and she wanted a front row seat when stuff got real.

When Maddie reached the window, though, Nazeerah didn't seem fired up. Instead, she looked sad and hopeless. She bowed her head and turned away from the Sultan. "Yes, Father," she said, meekly.

Maddie was heartbroken. She knew this wasn't what Nazeerah wanted. Maddie became even more determined to help her get out of marrying Haroun.

"Very well, then," the Sultan said. "See that this guest list gets to the head of staff."

Maddie watched as the Sultan placed a scroll on the table next to Nazeerah. That was exactly what Maddie was looking for! If Nazeerah couldn't put a stop to the wedding, their only hope was for Maddie to get Aladdin's name on the guest list. Then, he could stop the wedding himself!

Now was the perfect time to snatch the scroll. Nazeerah had her head in her hands, crying, and the Sultan was on his way out of the room. Neither of them was paying attention. Quietly, Maddie crept toward the table, reaching her arm up to snatch the scroll.

"Wait!" Nazeerah said, just as the Sultan reached the doorway. She looked up at her father, defiantly. Maddie had to dive under the table to avoid being seen.

"Yes, my sweet?" the Sultan said, turning around.

"Father, you should know that I — I met someone else!"

Yes! Maddie thought. Nazeerah's standing up for herself after all!

The Sultan closed the door. He spoke in a hushed voice, and Maddie couldn't quite tell whether he was angry. "What do you mean?" he asked.

"A man," Nazeerah said. "I've met a man, and I enjoy spending time with him." Maddie hid under the table, pumping her fist with excitement. This was it! They were on their way to the happy ending!

"A man?" The Sultan put his hands on his hips, defiantly. Nazeerah seemed to be losing her courage.

"He's very nice," Nazeerah said. "Nicer than Haroun!"

"Have you fallen in love with this man?" the Sultan asked.

"Well . . . well . . . ," Nazeerah stammered. Maddie was practically applauding, she was so excited. "I don't know," Nazeerah said.

Huh? Maddie was confused. She was supposed to be in love. If she wasn't, it was Holden's fault for being such a creep.

"I'm not sure I know what love is yet, but I'd like to find out. I'd like to postpone the wedding so I can have more time to think about this."

"This is quite a shock," the Sultan said. He began pacing back and forth across the room, trying to figure out what to do. "Of course, I want my daughter to be happy. Tell me, what is this prince's name?"

"Well . . ." Nazeerah shuffled her feet uncomfortably. "He's not exactly a prince."

"Not a prince?!" the Sultan thundered. "You're suggesting you want to call off your wedding to Prince Haroun for a . . . a . . . commoner?"

"I– I– ," Nazeerah stammered, unsure how to respond.

"How could a commoner ever become sultan when I someday step down? How would he know how to lead the kingdom?"

"But Father!"

"I am not just your father. I am your sultan! And you will do as I command! Tomorrow, you shall marry Prince Haroun, like it or not!"

Nazeerah wept as her father stormed out of the room.

Rats, Maddie thought. She was going to have to go back to her original plan: get Aladdin's name on the guest list, and hope Geeno did his part in making Holden want to come.

Right now was the perfect time to make her move, while Nazeerah was distracted with her own crying.

Maddie quietly crept out from under the table, reached up, and grabbed the scroll. She was so excited to have her hands on it, she called out, "Yes!"

Oops.

Nazeerah looked up to see who had spoken, and she saw Maddie the monkey holding the scroll with the guest list.

"Hey! What are you doing?"

Maddie froze. She was caught. Nazeerah was staring right at her, bending over to take back the scroll. Then, Maddie did the only thing she could think of to get out of this situation.

She tightened her grip on the scroll and ran as fast as she could.

Chapter 13

The Genie found Holden sitting in a large chair that tilted backward when he pulled a lever. The chair's arms each had holes in them, in which Holden had put a tall, thin green can of something called an "energy drink." From his reclined state, he held an oddly shaped hand controller covered with different-colored buttons. He stared at an enormous flat brown canvas that projected moving images, and he yelled things like, "Aw yeah!" and "Take that!" and "Blam blam blam!"

It struck Geeno in that moment that he didn't understand a single thing he had conjured for this strange boy.

"Hey, Genie, I wish you'd move about three feet to the side." Holden craned his neck, trying to see around Geeno.

"Sorry," Geeno said, stepping aside. He tried to think of how to express the confusion he was feeling in a way this boy might understand. "What heck you doing?"

"I'm playing *Splatter Battalion 6*. They say it's 90 percent gorier than *Splatter Battalion 5*. Wanna hop on multiplayer?"

Geeno was even more confused. "What talking about?" He looked at the screen, as a muscular man blasted the head off a drooling zombie with a gun the size of an overgrown elephant. "This horrible."

"You sound like my mom. She thinks it's too violent. Pfft!" On screen, Holden threw a grenade that blasted a whole horde of zombies into tiny, bloody pieces. He pumped his fist. "Yeah!"

The genie was so repulsed he had to shield his face. "Can wish for genie not throw up please?"

"Oh, come on," Holden said. "It's just a bunch of zeroes and ones in a computer program. It's not like they're real."

"Look real to Geeno."

"Trust me. Play for a few minutes, and you'll get desensitized." Holden tossed Geeno a gadget like the one he was holding, and a voice rang out from the screen, "Player two has joined the elimination squad!"

"What do now?" Geeno fretted, overwhelmed by the controller.

"Conjure yourself a chair and push some buttons."

Soon, the genie was sitting in a chair just like Holden's, trying to figure out the game they were playing. First, he pressed the green button on his controller. It fired a gun. Next, he pressed the red button. That fired a different gun. Then, he tried the blue button, which fired both guns at the same time. Last, he tried the yellow button, which fired both guns and simultaneously delivered a karate kick that knocked a zombie's head off.

"No! I sorry I hurt you!" he said, as the zombie's head rolled into a ditch and got devoured by a rabid werewolf.

"Fine," Holden sighed. "If you're going to be such a baby about it, we'll switch to puppy mode."

Geeno smiled. "Puppy mode? That sound nice!" Holden pulled up an on-screen menu and adjusted a few of the settings. Soon, all the zombies had changed into adorable puppies. They frolicked playfully in a field, rolling on their backs and pawing at butterflies.

Geeno giggled. "Oh, so cute."

Holden pressed some buttons, and suddenly, his mercenary character parachuted into the middle of the field. He opened fire on the puppies, who ran away, whimpering and scrambling for cover.

"Take that! *Sayonara*, sucka!" Holden laughed, as he blasted the puppies to smithereens.

Geeno put the controller down, unable to play anymore. He was starting to think Holden's mother was a very wise woman not to let him play games like this. Then, he got an idea. He waved his hands, and the puppies on screen grew to ten times their size. They were armed with gigantic guns, too, and driving a tank. With one enormous blast, they knocked Holden's character off the field, and a *Game over* screen came up.

"Hey!" Holden protested. "No fair using magic to beat me."

"What?" Geeno said, innocently. "They just zeroes and ones. Why play game anyway? Better go to banquet maybe?"

"Banquet? You mean Nazeerah's little wedding thing? No thanks. That's exactly the nonsense I try to avoid in these fairy tales. I hate that junk."

Geeno thought harder. He had to find a way to persuade Holden to go. "Come on, it be fun," he insisted. "They have dancing!"

"I hate dancing," Holden replied.

"They have people you meet!"

Holden rolled his eyes. "Fairy tale characters, talking about dresses and weddings and cute little talking animals you just want to squash under your foot!"

"They have food!"

"My food's better." He dipped a mozzarella stick in tomato sauce and ripped off a big chunk with his teeth. "Forget it, Genie. You're not going to get me to go to that boring banquet."

Holden pressed the start button and waited for his game to load. Geeno sighed. It was no use. He couldn't think of any way he could convince this kid to go to Nazeerah's wedding banquet.

Geeno took another look at the game Holden was playing as he left the room. Now, there were puppy zombies on screen. Geeno stopped short, getting an idea.

"You right. Don't go banquet. You just kid."

"Just a kid? Excuse me!" Holden said. "I'm your master!"

"Right, but you master no want you go."

"My master? I don't have a master."

"Oh yes. Her name 'Mom.'"

"Mom?"

"Yes. Her. Mom not want you go banquet. That sure."

"She wouldn't?"

"No, too grown up for boy like you." Geeno started to walk away. He only got about two steps.

"Wait!" Holden cried out.

"Yes?" Geeno said, turning back around.

Holden threw down his video game controller and stood up. "I'm going to this banquet!"

Geeno smiled and breathed a deep sigh of relief.

Chapter 14

Maddie scurried through the palace as quickly as her tiny monkey legs could carry her. Nazeerah was proving to be a surprisingly good runner, and she was gaining fast. At least now Maddie could run on two legs again, although it didn't help that she kept tripping over her long, curly tail. She wasn't sure how much longer she could put up with this chase. She was starting to run out of breath, and this hallway seemed to go on forever!

"Stop that monkey!" Nazeerah yelled.

"Yes, Your Highness!" a guard called back to her. Maddie looked up just in time to see the guard lunge toward her. She leapt out of the way with barely a moment to spare, and he missed her by less than an inch — a dangerously close call.

"I'll get him, Your Highness!" said another servant.

As Maddie looked in the woman's direction, she felt a huge *whack*! The servant swatted her with a broom and sent her flying.

"EEEEE!" Maddie screeched. She plummeted to the ground. Thinking fast, she curled up in a ball, hoping to dull the impact. She landed with a thud and went rolling down the hallway like a bowling ball. By now, servants were diving left and right to try to nab her. Maddie had to jump back and forth to dodge them.

She knew it was only a matter of time before someone grabbed her. Finally, she spotted an open doorway. This was her chance! She skidded through it, hoping it would provide an escape route.

"Oh no!" a servant shouted. "It's headed for the ballroom!"

Sure enough, Maddie found herself inside a massive ballroom, which was being set up for an elegant wedding banquet. Before she knew it, she was headed full-speed toward a long table pristinely arranged with fine china. It was a dead end! What could she do?

Thinking fast, Maddie planted the end of the scroll into the floor and used it to pole vault up onto the table. Clink! Dishes went flying everywhere, and all the servants who had been chasing Maddie were now falling over themselves trying to prevent the priceless china from crashing to the floor.

Maddie hoped that would distract everyone enough that she could get away, but she noticed one person still staring her down, dead set on catching her: Nazeerah. Maddie looked to her left, her right, in front and behind her, but there was no good way to run. Then, as if by instinct, she looked up. Now, she saw an option — a massive chandelier adorned with sparkling jewels. It was way out of reach, but she had to try.

Using the scroll to vault up once again, Maddie leapt as high as she could and stretched her furry, noodly arms desperately above her. Sadly, all she caught within her clutching fingers was air. She began falling back down, headfirst. Underneath her, Nazeerah waited with outstretched arms to catch her, a victorious smile on her face. Maddie closed her eyes and braced herself for capture.

Then, suddenly, she stopped.

She opened her eyes and realized she was no longer falling. She was suspended in mid-air, high over Nazeerah's head and far out of her reach. Was it magic? Was she flying?

No, it was her tail. Maddie looked over her shoulder and saw her long monkey tail had wrapped itself around one of the chandelier's arms, saving her. Relieved, Maddie swung across the ceiling, from one chandelier to the next, as if they were vines in the jungle. Jewels rained down onto the banquet tables, causing chaos throughout the ballroom.

"That monkey is ruining our wedding!" came a furious voice. A hush fell over the servants as Prince Haroun marched into the room. He crossed the dance floor in a fury, shaking his fist at Maddie.

It was then that Maddie noticed something very strange. Nazeerah was no longer trying to stop her. She was watching her, smiling. She actually seemed happy to see the preparations destroyed. Of course. She didn't want this wedding! Maddie started having fun, throwing gems from the chandelier onto tables to cause as much damage as possible. She smashed up centerpieces and obliterated champagne glasses. Maddie thought at one point she saw Nazeerah wink at her.

Haroun's rage was only growing in intensity. "Bring me its head!" he spat, viciously.

Nazeerah gasped, and Maddie gulped in horror.

Servants climbed atop the banquet tables in hopes of reaching Maddie. They stretched and leapt, and some of them came close enough to touch her fur. Maddie scanned the room. Her first priority now was getting out of there. She spotted an open window high on a far wall. It was so far, further than she could possibly leap. She had to get closer — and fast. She was losing her grip on the chandelier and would soon fall right into Haroun's arms.

"Hurry, servants!" Haroun hissed. "I'll not have my big day ruined by a filthy ape!"

Maddie couldn't reach the window from the chandelier, but she realized that if she tried hard enough, she might be able to bring the chandelier closer to the window. She swayed her body back and forth, and the mighty chandelier began to swing.

Whatever jewels were still left on the massive fixture were soon shaken free, and servants scrambled to avoid being hit. Maddie swung the chandelier harder and harder, until it was as close as it could get to the window. Then, with no other means to flee, she took a deep breath, let go, and went hurtling through the air. Just as she reached the window and managed to grasp onto it by the very tip of her fingernails, she heard a tremendous rattling.

The chandelier had ripped from its mounting. As Maddie watched in shock, the entire hulking structure came loose and plummeted to the floor. Haroun dove out of the way just in time, but there was no saving the chandelier. It shattered into a million pieces, taking out half a dozen tables with it and sending debris all over the room.

"Whoa," Maddie whispered, as she realized the damage she had done. Her hand started to slip, so she turned her attention back to the window and used all her might to pull herself up and outside to freedom.

"Curse you, Monkey!" Haroun shouted from beside a pile of rubble, as his primate nemesis disappeared from view.

Maddie found herself on a tiny ledge, high above the palace courtyard. She was able to leap from there to a palm tree and then shimmy down its trunk. It felt good to be back on solid ground, safe and sound. Being a monkey was kind of fun! She was good at it, too! She had the scroll, and she was free, totally free!

At least, she thought she was, until a shadow fell over her and soft footsteps approached.

"Why would you do all of that just for a little scroll, Monkey?" Maddie looked up at Nazeerah, who had her cornered against the palace wall.

She was definitely trapped now. She couldn't run. She couldn't hide. All she could do was reason with Nazeerah.

"Because I don't think you should marry Prince Haroun," Maddie replied. "You can do better!"

"AAAAAH!" Nazeerah screamed. "A talking monkey!"

Oh, right. For a moment, Maddie forgot she was an animal. Now, she'd freaked out the princess once again. As Nazeerah backed away, Maddie saw an opportunity to get free, so she ran off with the scroll.

Finally, she had what she came for, but she had no idea what to do next.

Chapter 15

Princess Nazeerah staggered through the courtyard of her palace, taking deep breaths to calm herself down. Was she imagining things, or were animals really starting to talk?

It was strange enough on its own, but what was truly odd was that the particular animals who'd been reaching out to her had been making so much sense. Both the camel and the monkey seemed to think she should call off the wedding to Prince Haroun, and they made some really good points. Haroun was cold and domineering. He insisted on having his way. Aladdin was fun and interesting to talk to. Life with him would be wild and unpredictable.

It was such a big decision, though. She couldn't make it alone.

"Excuse me," she said. "Do you think Aladdin is my true love?" She perched over a dove that was splashing in a fountain and waited for it to respond. "Hello?"

The dove continued frolicking, and Nazeerah grew impatient. She turned to face a snake charmer. "Will my father ever forgive me if I call off my wedding to Haroun?"

The snake charmer stopped playing his tune and tried to answer her. "Well, that's a very difficult question."

"Not you!" Nazeerah snapped, turning toward the snake. "What do you think?"

"Sssssssss," said the snake, curling back up inside his basket.

"Why won't anyone answer me?" Nazeerah asked. She ran through the courtyard, waving her arms madly at every animal she saw — mice, cats, even a beetle. "Hello? You? Somebody help me!"

It was no use. Now that she needed the wise counsel of a talking animal, there was none to be found. Unable to get a response, she returned to the palace to see what had become of the ballroom. The scope of the devastation was greater than she could have imagined. Everything was destroyed, and what should have been the most opulent banquet in the kingdom's history was left in ruins. She couldn't believe one little monkey was capable of doing so much damage, and the thought of it brought a smile back to her face.

Maybe she wouldn't need to call off the wedding after all. There was no way anyone would be able to celebrate with the entire banquet hall laid to waste like this.

That's when she saw Haroun, sifting through the debris, in despair. "Have you spoken to my father yet?" she asked him. "We'll have to cancel the wedding, naturally."

"The wedding shall go on!" Haroun declared. Nazeerah stared at him in disbelief, as did everyone else within earshot. Surely, he couldn't be serious.

"But how?" the Sultan asked, stepping into the room. He was nearly in tears to see a part of his palace in such a shambles. "Everything is ruined! There's no way we'll be ready in time."

"It will go on, but as a private ceremony," Haroun explained. "Just the princess and me. No banquet, no ball, no guests. Just us expressing our love and our desire to stay together for all eternity." He winked at Nazeerah, but she retreated in despair. Haroun sensed her dislike, but that only strengthened his resolve. "And it shall happen tonight!" he shouted.

With that, Haroun brushed himself off and marched out of the ballroom.

"Nazeerah," the Sultan said, laying his hand on her shoulder. But the princess couldn't bear to speak to her father at that moment. She pulled away and ran straight to her room, closing herself inside.

Maddie always prided herself on her neat penmanship, so she was disappointed to see what a scribbled mess her monkey hands made of the name Aladdin on the guest list. It was worse than Holden's handwriting, which their teacher, Mrs. Greenberg, once described as "a toddler trying to write in Martian." Oh well. After she destroyed the ballroom, what were the odds the wedding would still take place?

"Have you heard?" a voice whispered from down the hall. "The wedding is still taking place!"

Huh? Maddie's ears perked up at the sound of the women talking.

"Oh no!" another woman replied. "Where's the guest list?"

Maddie gasped and grabbed the scroll. She followed the sound of the women's voices down the hallway, eager to get it to them.

"It doesn't matter," said another woman. "There won't be any guests. Prince Haroun has declared it a private ceremony."

Maddie gasped again. She peered through a doorway and saw the servants talking in the palace kitchen.

"It's so sad," another woman said. "Poor Princess Nazeerah just sits in her room and cries."

Maddie dropped the scroll. She wouldn't be needing it now. She had to get to Nazeerah instead.

Nazeerah's door was locked, but Maddie was able to scamper onto a ledge outside the princess's window so she could see her. Sure enough, Nazeerah laid on her bed, crying. She was all alone, but occasionally, Maddie heard her talking to herself. "I wish my father would listen to me!" she wailed. "I wish I'd never met Haroun!" "I wish I could marry who I wanted!" Just hearing it broke Maddie's heart. She wanted to help Nazeerah, but once again, she felt helpless. A monkey might be able to steal a scroll, even trash a ballroom, but how could one ever save a princess?

It was then that she heard a soft buzzing sound. It was oddly familiar, like the sound of something moving, but she couldn't recall where she had heard it before. Then, there was another sound. It was a man's voice, singing. Horribly.

From her perch, Maddie could see the front gate of the palace, where a young man rode up on a flying skateboard.

"In your eyes, I see pancakes, with syrup and some toast!" Holden and Geeno hovered toward the palace gates, side by side on matching hoverboards and dressed for a wedding. "I take it back," Holden said, kicking his hoverboard up and tucking it under his arm. "Give it some better lyrics, and that song is kinda catchy."

Maddie scampered down to them, waving her arms. "Holden! You made it!"

"Yeah, I felt bad for Nazeerah," he said. "This party would've been so lame without me."

"Well, I have some bad news," Maddie said. "Haroun called it off."

"He called off the wedding?" Holden asked.

"No, just the party. Nazeerah's in her room, miserable. She just lies in bed, making one wish after another."

"Maybe she needs some time alone," Holden said, turning his hoverboard around.

"She need genie," Geeno said. He looked over his shoulder at Holden and added, "Genie never go to right people."

"Hey, I get it! That was directed at me!" Holden said. "Wasn't it?"

"You have been awfully hard on your genie," Maddie said.

"And you make stepsister monkey. That mean," Geeno agreed.

"I just wanted to have some fun," Holden said. "I'm not a bad guy."

"Actually, you are a bad guy," Maddie said. "Everything that's gone wrong in this story has been because of you. You won't marry Nazeerah. You're totally selfish, just doing everything you want. You don't treat the genie like a real person."

"Hey, that's not fair!" Holden said. "I'm great to the genie."

"Oh yeah?" Geeno said. "What my name?"

"I know your name," Holden retorted. "It's . . ." He looked at the genie, having no clue what his name was. He gritted his teeth under Maddie's withering glare and decided to take a guess. "Mitch?" he said. Maddie groaned. "No, I meant Mike! Uh, Christopher!"

"My name Geeno."

"Really?" Holden scratched his head. "That sounds a lot like Genie."

"It totally different!" Geeno said, turning his back on Holden.

"Aw, man. I should've kept guessing. I would've gotten there eventually."

"Nice work, Holden," Maddie explained. "This is the worst you've ever behaved. I think you're the bad guy in this story."

"I'm not the bad guy!" Holden insisted. "I know I'm not!"

"Really? Have you checked your tablet lately?" Maddie asked.

"My tablet? Oh yeah!" Holden pulled the tablet out of his coat and clicked on the eBook of *Aladdin*. "Here it is," he said. "*Aladd–*"

He stopped short as soon as he saw the title page. It was different than it had been earlier. Now, it featured an evil-looking Aladdin, riding on a hoverboard, with Geeno, Nazeerah, and a monkey cowering behind him.

"Is that me? Wait, that can't be right," he said.

He flipped through the pages and saw more pictures that made him look bad. Him running the genie ragged. Him cackling as he turned Maddie into a monkey. Him boring Nazeerah with an air guitar solo on the magic carpet.

"I don't believe it," he said. "I *am* the bad guy."

Holden put the tablet away, sulking. Maddie and the genie shared a concerned look.

Maddie rested a hand on Holden's shoulder, consoling him. "You're not that bad," she said. "You came to the wedding, right?"

"Only because I thought my mom wouldn't want me to," he said. "I haven't done anything nice for anybody else in this whole story."

"Well, I'm afraid it's too late now." Maddie shook her head. "Haroun and Nazeerah are going to get married, and there's nothing we can do to stop it."

"Yes, there is," Holden said. "Nazeerah needs a genie? Well, I'm going to give her one."

Maddie and Nazeerah looked up at him, hopeful. "Holden, that's a brilliant idea!" Maddie said.

"Thanks," Holden said. "And you're going to be a great genie."

"What?" Maddie asked. "Me?"

"Geeno, make my stepsister a genie," Holden declared.

"Wait, really?" Maddie said.

"You don't like being a monkey, right? Geeno, do it!"

"As wish," Geeno replied. He waved his hands, and Maddie began to panic.

"Holden, you're not really going to make me a—" With a mighty whoosh, a wind swept Maddie off her feet and transformed her into a floating specter. "No!" she protested. "No!" Maddie tossed and flailed as she shrunk down and funneled into a polished metal lamp.

Even when she was inside it, the lamp rattled from her protests.

"Now, go leave that thing where Nazeerah will find it," Holden said to Geeno. "I'll wait here."

"As wish," Geeno said. He picked up the lamp, struggling to hold onto it as Maddie thrashed about inside. Everywhere she turned, she seemed to bump into something. She took one step to her right. THUD! One step back to the left. THUD! She reached her hands over her head, and before she could fully extend her arms, they both bumped into the ceiling. THUD! THUD! It didn't help that it was pitch dark inside the lamp and she couldn't see anything.

"Psst! Psst!" Geeno's voice came from above, as he whispered through the lamp's tiny opening. "Stop struggling. I drop you!"

"Ugh!" Maddie let out a huge groan, then stopped fighting against the fact that she was now a genie, trapped in a lamp. "It's so cramped in here!" she complained.

Geeno shrugged. "Get used to it after thousand years," he explained.

Maddie felt the lamp begin to shake and sway. "What's going on?" she asked.

"We outside Nazeerah room," Geeno said. "I leave lamp here."

"Hopefully, she'll find me soon," Maddie said. "I kind of have to pee."

Geeno shook his head. "Should've done that before sucked into lamp."

"Wait, what?" Maddie asked. "What? Geeno?"

Geeno placed the lamp down and floated away. If he'd bothered to look in the room, he would've noticed that Nazeerah was no longer inside.

Holden stared at the tablet screen. It pained him to see Aladdin drawn as a bad guy, but now that he had set his brilliant plan in motion, he expected the illustrations to change any moment. He flipped to the picture of him waiting outside the palace gates and wondered what would appear. Nazeerah rushing into his arms? Maddie with a big goofy genie head? He saw a face getting sketched in behind him. It didn't look like Nazeerah or Maddie. It looked like a man.

"What are you doing at this castle?" a voice raged.

Holden turned around and saw whom the picture was sketching. It was Prince Haroun, and he was furious.

Holden decided to play it cool. He quickly slipped the tablet back in his coat. "I heard there was a wedding today, so what's up?"

"Oh, there's a wedding," Haroun huffed. "The most beautiful woman in the world will be marrying the man of her dreams, me!"

"Nice, then I'll just go see if I can score a good seat." Holden tried to enter the palace, but Haroun stepped into his path to block him.

"You're not invited. This is a private affair. Just me and my bride."

"That doesn't sound too fun."

"It's not supposed to be fun. It's supposed to be royal. That means no riff-raff, no street urchins, no classless clowns. I deserve only the best!"

"Get over yourself, Haroun!" said a voice behind them.

Both men turned around as Princess Nazeerah stepped out of the palace, shaking her head.

"You've come out of your room!" Haroun said.

"I saw through the window that Aladdin was waiting outside to see me. I wanted to hear what he had to say."

"Very well, then," Haroun said. He turned angrily toward Holden. "So what do you have to say?"

Holden looked back and forth between Haroun and Nazeerah. He figured he should say something romantic, but he couldn't think of anything. Besides, Haroun was very big and very angry. "Just, y'know . . . wuzzup?"

Nazeerah hung her head, disappointed. Haroun laughed mockingly. "Well, now that you're out of your room, let's begin the wedding." Haroun grabbed Nazeerah by the hand and started to walk her back inside.

"Wait," she said. She let go of Haroun's hand and turned back toward Aladdin. "Would you like to come be our witness?"

Haroun fumed. "You must be joking!"

"He came all the way across the kingdom on his . . . ," she looked at the hoverboard quizzically, "magic floating plank thing. So if he wants to join us, he should be able to. It's my wedding, too!" She stared defiantly into Haroun's eyes. He was still furious, but he backed down.

"Fine! Let's just get this over with!" he said, stomping back into the palace.

None of them noticed, but from a balcony up above them, the Sultan had witnessed the entire scene. He nodded quietly as he watched Nazeerah lead Holden back inside the palace.

Chapter 16

Maddie stretched and repositioned herself over and over again until she was able to find a comfortable sitting position inside the lamp. It was worse than the day she went snow tubing with her cousins on pay-by-the-carload day, and she had to cram into the backseat with six other girls in parkas.

Once she was off her feet, she did her best to relax, resolving that she wouldn't move again until the lamp found its new master. She wasn't sure how much time had gone by. One moment, she thought she had only been inside for a few seconds. Then, the next, she imagined that it had been a thousand years. She wondered if she'd emerge to find herself living in a future where people rode in flying cars and had robots for pets.

(She was right the first time. It had been twenty-six seconds.)

Before long, she heard footsteps approaching. She sat up, bursting with anticipation. Not only was she about to get out of this tiny space, but she'd emerge as a genie, with amazing magical powers. She'd be able to help Nazeerah out of her predicament and make sure the story had a happy ending. Then would come the best part of all. She'd go back home, back to her parents and her slumber party, and back to being herself.

"How dare she humiliate me!" a voice echoed from outside the lamp. Sound didn't travel well through the tiny opening, but Maddie thought it sounded like a man's voice. Was that possible? The genie put the lamp by Nazeerah's room, so naturally she would be the one to open it. Yes, it had to be Nazeerah. It was probably just the strange acoustics in the lamp that were warping the voice to make it seem deeper.

"What's this?" the voice continued. "A lamp?"

Maddie smiled. Everything was going according to plan.

"Hmm . . . looks like a magic lamp!" the voice said. Swish, swish! Maddie got knocked back and forth, and she realized only one thing could possibly be happening. Nazeerah was rubbing the lamp. Soon, she felt a tingling throughout her body. Light streamed into the lamp, and Maddie could feel herself getting sucked out, where she at last was face-to-face with her new master . . .

Haroun!?

"No, you weren't supposed to find the lamp!" Maddie said as she floated above him.

Haroun let rip an evil cackle. "Oh, but I did, and that makes me your master. Now, let's get started. I have so many things to wish for! BA-HAHAHAHAHAHA!"

Holden didn't usually like peaceful things like gardens and quiet, but he enjoyed the calm as Nazeerah led him through the palace courtyard. There were bushes that had been trimmed into fancy shapes, doves flapping playfully in birdbaths, and trees with all different kinds of fruit. Even though they were in the middle of the desert, there was a soft mist coming from a waterfall that kept the temperature bearable.

"That was awesome how you talked smack to the prince," Holden said. "He's such a loser."

"I don't know about that," Nazeerah replied. "He wins every argument we have."

"No, I mean he's a ding-dong," Holden said. "A stinker, a lame-o, a creepface." He could see from Nazeerah's expression that she didn't understand any of these terms. "I mean, I don't like him."

Nazeerah nodded sadly. "Neither do I."

"Then why are you marrying him?" Holden asked.

"I don't have a choice. I have to marry a prince." She turned toward him. "I only wish you could be a prince."

Holden groaned. "Oh, but it sounds so awful. The outfits princes wear, the stuff they do. All that royal lameness bores me. Maybe there's another way to get out of this. Maybe instead of me becoming royalty, you could quit."

"Quit? Quit what?"

"Quit being a princess. Ditch the palace and the responsibilities. Come hang out with me instead."

"But what would we do?"

"Whatever we want! You wouldn't have to listen to your dad anymore."

Nazeerah thought about this for a long time. It was a huge decision. Finally, she took a deep breath. "Yes!" Nazeerah shouted, gleefully. "Yes! That sounds fun!"

"Sweet!" Holden said. "Nazeerah, you're pretty cool!"

Nazeerah gazed deeply into Holden's eyes. Her lips turned upward in a half-smile. He smiled back, but then he started to think how strange it was that Nazeerah was still looking at him. This was a long time to look at someone and not say something. What exactly was she seeing in his eyes that was so interesting?

Then Holden remembered that nutty song. This was romantic for her! She could be seeing anything in his eyes — double cheeseburgers, two-headed llamas, all kinds of cool stuff. Slowly, Nazeerah started to lean toward him, and Holden was gripped by panic.

Was she trying to kiss him? Yuck!

Holden looked around for the genie so he could wish his way out of this. Maybe he could wish to have his lips disappear or to develop a wicked case of stink breath. Oh, man. Why did he have to send the genie away?

"Holden! Holden!" An urgent voice came from nearby. It shook Nazeerah out of her love gaze, saving Holden for the moment.

"Who is that?" Holden asked, and two twinkling bodies rose up above the hedge maze. He looked at them in shock. "Maddie?"

Maddie floated down to him in a hurry, with Geeno following behind her. Nazeerah was shocked. "Two genies?"

"Yeah, I conjured one for you," Holden said. "Now you can wish to marry who you want!"

"No she can't!" Maddie said. "She didn't find me, so I'm not her genie."

"What?"

"Holden, there's no time to explain. I need you to wish to be the best swordsman in the kingdom."

"Why?" Holden asked.

"Do this!" Geeno demanded. "Hurry!"

"Fine, I wish to be the best swordsman in the kingdom," Holden said.

The genie waved his arms, and a sharp scimitar appeared by Holden's side. He had never seen such a long, curved sword before, but when he picked it up, it felt totally natural in his hands. "Now what?" he asked.

Before anyone could answer, a voice rang out from across the garden. "Aladdin, I challenge you to a duel for the princess's hand in marriage!"

Holden looked around for the source of the voice. "Who's that?"

"My master," Maddie admitted, sheepishly.

A massive figure emerged, stomping across the hedges and flattening each of them under his feet. He was ten feet tall and he held a shining scimitar of his own. It took Holden a moment to recognize him, but when he held up his sword to fight, he knew for sure this was Prince Haroun.

"*En garde!*" the prince said. Holden trembled with fear as Haroun held out his sword and lunged toward him.

Chapter 17

The hulking Prince Haroun raced across the garden with his sword drawn. As Holden watched the blade grow closer, aimed directly for his neck, he did the only thing he could think to do.

He screamed. "AAAAAAAAAH!"

But also, he swung his own sword. It happened so fast, so effortlessly, he barely realized he had done it. He simply heard the clang of metal against metal and watched Haroun stumble aside as he deflected the blow.

"Wow, I *am* a good swordsman!" Holden announced, posing proudly with his blade.

"Holden, watch out!" Maddie screamed. Her stepbrother turned just in time to see Haroun racing toward him. Once more, Holden was able to deflect the blade at the last second.

"Okay, he's pretty good, too," Holden admitted.

"He wished to be the best swordsman in the kingdom right before you did," Maddie whispered.

"Ah, I get it!" Holden said. "I was the last one to wish for it, so I'm the best."

"Well, I wish to be the best swordsman again!" Haroun declared.

Maddie waved her arms to make it happen. "Sorry, Holden. I have to."

"You think you're so smart?" Holden said. "Well, now I wish to be the best swordsman again!"

Geeno waved his arms, and Holden felt his strength grow.

"Now I wish it!" Haroun said.

"Now I do!" Holden said.

"Me!"

"Me!"

"Me, me, me, me, me!"

"Me times infinity!"

"Me times infinity squared!"

"Hey, I thought you only got three wishes," Holden said.

"As if I don't know the infinite wish loophole!" Haroun replied. "Hmph!"

Maddie and Geeno looked at each other and shrugged, neither of them sure what to do.

"I have an idea," Nazeerah said, stepping between the two swordsmen. "How about you put down your arms. I do not want any bloodshed in my name!"

"Very well, Princess," Haroun said, resting his sword at his side.

"Really?" Holden said. "Hmm, maybe you're not such a bad guy after all." He, too, rested his sword at his side. He turned toward Nazeerah. "Okay, so then how do we settle this? Should we play Crazy Eights? You have a deck of cards?"

"RWAAAAAAAR!" thundered Haroun. He picked up his sword and swiped toward Holden's chest.

"Ow!" Holden shouted. He looked down and saw a cut across his chest. He was bleeding. "No fair!" he shouted. "Cheater!" He grabbed his own sword and began to fight back.

"Stop!" Nazeerah demanded.

"No way," Holden said. "I'm totally gonna waste this guy." He and Haroun continued to clash blades, each blow with more force than the last. They parried and leapt across the garden. Holden only seemed to get better as the fight progressed. Soon, he was doing backflips to avoid the prince's advances.

"Whoo! I'm awesome!" he cheered.

Nazeerah had had enough. She stormed off angrily as the two men fought. Maddie wanted to let her stepbrother know that he was allowing the princess to slip away, but Holden was too wrapped up in the fight to pay attention.

They were both so good, Holden thought they might go on fighting forever. He needed something to turn the fight in his favor. That's when he saw his hoverboard lying nearby. All he had to do was get to it. "Hey, look! A three-humped camel!" he said, pointing behind Haroun.

"What?" Haroun said. He looked over his shoulder where Holden was pointing, and Holden raced across the garden. He hopped on his hoverboard and moved back in Haroun's direction.

"You may be a pretty good swordsman," he said, "but I bet you can't keep up with me on a hoverboard." Laughing, Holden hovered closer toward Haroun.

"I wish to be the best in the kingdom on a hoverboard!" Haroun said quickly.

"Rats!" Holden shouted, as Maddie waved her arms.

Soon, the two of them were continuing their swordfight while floating on hoverboards, tricking off walls and fountains. Holden knew that at any instant, he could get fatally slashed with Haroun's blade, but he couldn't help feeling like this was also the coolest thing that had ever happened.

He fought hard, and he didn't give up. Soon, he could tell he was overpowering Haroun. He felt like a character in *Splatter Batallion 6*. A new class, called a hover-fighter. All he needed was the perfect finishing move to take his opponent out, something twisted and disgusting like the characters would do in the game. He lunged for his opponent, but in his excitement, he slipped. He fell off his hoverboard, tumbling to the ground, and on his way, he only managed a small slice across Haroun's right cheek.

"Ouch!" Haroun whined. Holden picked himself up off the ground, checking out the cut he had given to his opponent. It was bleeding a lot. Holden wanted to feel the rush of victory, but instead, he was struck by the queasiness of nausea. He could stomach watching horrific dismemberments in his video game, but in real life, a simple flesh wound made him want to throw up. It looked really painful, and he didn't feel like he had won anything. He felt bad for hurting this guy.

"Whoa, dude," Holden said, leaning over Haroun. "I'm sorry, that looks like it really hurts. You okay?"

"No," Haroun cried, lying meekly on the ground. "I have been defeated. You have won the right to finish me off." Haroun closed his eyes and braced himself so that Holden could stab him with his sword.

"Are you mental?" Holden said, tossing his sword aside. "I'm not going to kill you." Holden extended his hand to help Haroun to his feet. Overcome with emotion, Haroun grabbed hold and stood up.

Maddie and Geeno breathed a sigh of relief that the fight was over. Holden bent down to pick up his hoverboard. "Dude, have you ever played video games? You'd be an awesome co-op partner."

As Maddie watched in horror, Haroun's gaze grew cold once again. Seeing Holden bent over, he reached for his sword, raised it up high, and prepared to bring it down with all his might.

"Holden! Look out!" Maddie screamed.

But it was too late. Holden's sword was out of reach, and Haroun had already begun to strike the final blow.

Chapter 18

Holden cowered on the floor, helpless as Haroun swung his scimitar. There wasn't even time to wish his way out of this. He was doomed for sure.

Then, just as the blade was about to make its cold, piercing contact with Holden's body, another sword appeared. With a mighty "Yawhh!" someone swiped Haroun's scimitar out of the way. In one single, masterful move, a mysterious swordfighter appeared, saving Holden and disarming Haroun at the same time. The two men both looked in awe to see who had made such a stunning entrance.

They found Princess Nazeerah, sword in hand, shaking her head at their foolishness. "I said I didn't want anyone fighting over me!" she scolded.

She had everyone's attention now. Maddie pumped her fist to cheer her on. She wasn't sure where this was taking the story, but she loved seeing this side of Nazeerah.

"Woohoo!" she cheered.

"No more magic for you!" Nazeerah said to Haroun as she held her sword to his neck. "Have your genie undo all of this at once."

Haroun sighed. "Fine, I wish you had never become my genie at all."

"As you wish!" Maddie said. She waved her arms, and a magic mist swirled all around them. Haroun shrunk down to his usual height, and Maddie gained her legs back, returning to her human form.

"Very well," Nazeerah said. She retracted her blade and allowed Haroun to stand back up. She then helped Holden to his feet. "I don't want to be a prize in a swordfight," she continued. "I'm not anyone's possession, or a helpless victim."

"How did you do that?" Holden asked. "How did you beat both of us in the fight?"

Nazeerah smiled. "Well clearly, neither of you swordsmen are as good as the kingdom's greatest swordswoman." She twirled her sword and tossed it high above her head, then backflipped across the room and caught it with her eyes closed.

"And I didn't have to wish myself good," she added. "I trained."

"You're awesome!" Maddie said.

"When I want something, I work hard for it. That's what I plan to do for the people of my kingdom. And that's why I've decided to marry . . ."

Everyone held their breath for the big decision. Maddie could feel it. This was the moment the story would get back on track and they'd be able to go home.

". . . no one!" Nazeerah announced.

Maddie gasped.

Holden looked at Nazeerah, hurt. "But I thought we had a thing!"

"I do have a lot of fun with you, but you can't play games forever. I wouldn't be happy playing all day and knowing my kingdom needed me."

Haroun snickered, shaking his head. "It doesn't matter what you think," he mocked Nazeerah. "You shall still be my wife. Your father is the sultan, and he's insisting upon it!"

"Not anymore!" Everyone turned and saw the Sultan standing in the doorway. He had been watching the entire scene. He brushed past Haroun dismissively and took his daughter's hand. "I wanted my daughter to marry a prince so that I could step down from the throne and crown a new sultan, someone who knew how to lead. Now I see that there's no better leader than my daughter herself. I was hoping she would show me that she has the courage and self-confidence to make difficult decisions. Now I know that she does. She doesn't need a sultan. She will make a perfect sultana."

Nazeerah threw her arms around the Sultan and gave him a loving hug. "Thank you, Father!"

"The party will go on," the Sultan announced, "but not as a wedding. As a coronation! Today, I will step down from the throne, and crown Sultana Nazeerah!"

"Good luck!" Haroun sneered. "The wedding hall has been destroyed."

"Then the party will be in the streets of the kingdom, and everyone will be invited!" the Sultan declared. He cocked an eyebrow toward Prince Haroun. "Everyone, except you."

Chapter 19

Nazeerah's coronation was just as magical and jubilant as Maddie would've expected . . . with a few minor differences.

For one thing, the grand buffet included mozzarella sticks and jalapeño poppers. For another, the sultana's arrival was announced by trumpeters who rode in on hoverboards. And most unexpected of all, the townspeople danced to a strange, loud style of music they'd never heard before.

"Good evening . . . um, wherever we are!" said the lead singer of Hashtag Number Sign, Nigel McFoodge, gazing around the fairy tale kingdom. The band had been touring the world for so long, and been through so many different cities, that they barely noticed they were now playing their hit songs in a fairy tale. As long as their fans were rocking out with them, they were happy to jam.

Everyone in the kingdom came out to share in the festivities. They were so thrilled to have such a kind, dedicated new sultana as Nazeerah that none of them seemed to mind that there wouldn't be a royal wedding after all.

Among the most honored guests were Maddie, Holden, and Geeno, who got to stand right behind the Sultana as she waved to the crowd.

"Well, that's one more happy ending, thanks to us," Holden said, proudly. "We're getting really good at this."

"I don't know," Maddie said. "If that's the happily ever after, then why haven't we been sent home yet?"

She looked beside her at Geeno, the only one in attendance without a smile on his face. That's when she realized what was missing.

Just then, the Sultan stepped forward to give a speech.

"My work as your sultan was never easy," he said, "but it was a walk in the park compared to my other job: being a parent."

He shared a smile with his daughter.

"I made so many difficult decisions, and so many times, my choices angered my daughter. But I always kept one goal in mind: to raise the best child I could and to prepare her to stand on her own when she was ready. I'm proud to say that that time has come."

Maddie looked at Holden, who was listening very closely. The Sultan's words made them both think about Holden's fight with Carol.

"Over the years, we had disagreements, and we had sorrows, but without them, we wouldn't be where we are now. To me, she will always be my little girl." He turned to Nazeerah, brushing her cheek gently with the back of his hand. "To her, I say thank you for all the joy you've given me and for working so hard to be yourself."

Then, he faced the hordes of royal subjects assembled throughout the square. "To the rest of you, I say . . . I now present your new sultana!"

The crowd erupted in cheers. Nazeerah held her father's hand as they gazed upon the adoring citizens. It seemed like the applause might continue forever, so finally, the Sultan waved his arms to get the jubilant masses to quiet down.

"Now, if the band could play us a song," he continued, "I'd like to have a dance with my daughter."

Holden whispered to Nigel, and Nigel nodded knowingly, signaling the rest of the band.

Together, Hashtag Number Sign launched into a tender ballad about all the beautiful things you could see in someone's eyes, and the former sultan and the new sultana began to dance.

There was hardly a dry eye in the kingdom by that point. Even Holden tried to hide his face so Maddie wouldn't see him tearing up. Not that she would've noticed, though. She and Geeno were blubbering openly, resting their heads on each other's shoulders.

Holden used the moment to take a peek at his tablet. There, he saw that the cover of the story had changed once again. Even the title was different now. *Nazeerah*, it read. Holden's face was in the background, along with Maddie's, Geeno's, and the face of the story's main villain, Prince Haroun.

"This beautiful!" Geeno gushed. "No one ever appreciate parents!"

"Fine, I get it!" Holden said. "I was a creep to my mom. So when can we get out of here?"

"I think there's one more thing you need to do," Maddie said, motioning toward Geeno.

Holden sighed. "I guess I was a creep to you, too. When somebody does everything you want them to, you kind of don't appreciate them."

"So . . . ?" the genie said, expectantly.

"So, Geeno, I wish you your freedom."

No sooner had Holden said the words than Geeno began to take his old shape again. He grew legs, and he went back to wearing the primitive clothes of a Neanderthal.

"Thank you," Geeno said. "You grant Geeno wish." Then, before Holden's eyes, Geeno began to fade from sight.

"What's happening now?" Holden asked.

"I going home," Geeno said, smiling. He then faded completely from view, and only a soft echo of his voice lingered in the air. "Just like you . . ."

"Like us?" Holden said. He glanced at Maddie and discovered that she was now fading, too, just like Geeno did. "Maddie?" Holden called out, as he watched his stepsister disappear into thin air. In disbelief, he turned to look at himself, but when he gazed down at his body, there was nothing there. He was already gone.

The next thing Maddie and Holden knew, they were back in the kitchen of their house. All the lights were out, and the entire home was so quiet they could hear the ticking of a clock from down the hall. Maddie peeked through the kitchen door and saw all her friends sound asleep in their sleeping bags, just as she'd left them.

"What a relief," she whispered to her stepbrother. "Nobody woke up while we were gone." When she turned around, she caught Holden sneaking a glance at his tablet. "Hey, what are you looking at?"

"Nothing!" Holden insisted, turning the screen off.

"Let me see," Maddie said. She grabbed the tablet and turned it back on. On the screen was an illustration showing Geeno reunited with his Neanderthal family. His wife and three young children all threw their arms around him, crying tears of joy. "Aw, you wanted to make sure Geeno was okay."

"No I didn't," Holden said, taking the tablet back. "Who cares?"

"Well, I know how much fun it was to get everything you wished for, so thanks for doing the right thing. You must be pretty bummed to be back home."

Holden looked up on the wall at a picture of his mom, and smiled to himself. "Yeah, consider it your birthday present."

"Hey, you know what?" Maddie jogged over to the fridge. "Your mom saved your cake for you. Should we?"

"I'm not really hungry," Holden said. "I had a lot of jalapeño poppers."

Maddie put the cake on the kitchen counter and started poking candles into the frosting. "You don't have to eat it," she said. "But you do have to make your birthday wish." Maddie lit the candles and pushed the cake toward Holden. "Go on!"

Holden shrugged and pushed the cake back toward Maddie. "Eh, I've made enough wishes today. Why don't you take it?"

Maddie nodded and leaned over the cake. "Okay, but I'm going to wish for something for you."

She inhaled deeply, then blew out all the candles with one breath.

"What did you wish for?" Holden asked.

"I can't tell you!"

"But it's my wish!"

"So? I still can't tell you," Maddie replied.

"Whatever," Holden said. He picked up the cake and returned it to the fridge. "Go back to your slumber party. It's pretty late."

Maddie looked at the clock. It was well past midnight. "Yeah. Hey, I guess you can call your dad in Germany now!"

"Yeah, I guess I can," Holden said.

"Good night," Maddie replied, as she left the room.

Holden was about to follow her out and head upstairs to his bedroom, when something caught his eye. There, on the kitchen counter, was the birthday present his mom got him. She had fished it out of the trash, brushed it off, and left it there for him. He stared at it for a moment, feeling guilty for the way he had acted. He probably should've just opened it, even if it was something lame.

Then again, what if it wasn't? What if his mom got him something really awesome to make up for the fact that she wasn't getting him a hoverboard? The curiosity was suddenly killing him. He couldn't wait until morning to find out. He grabbed the present and tore off the wrapping paper, revealing a small cardboard box.

What could it be inside? he wondered. A gift card to the hobby store? A download code for a new video game? Maybe it was the keys to a brand new, souped-up ATV that was waiting for him outside. Nah, knowing his mom, it was probably none of those things.

He nudged off the lid and discovered a folded-up piece of paper inside the box. That's it. Nothing exciting. Just a piece of paper. But when he unfolded it and held it up to the moonlight to read it, he realized it was something much more than that.

It was a plane ticket.

To Germany.

Holden stared at it for a long time, as if he wasn't even sure if it was real. It had a date, a seat number, even the price. For that money, his mom probably could've bought him the ATV. But he was glad she didn't. It was perfect. It was actually better than a hoverboard. If this was Maddie's birthday wish for him, she nailed it.

He heard footsteps approaching, so he quickly shoved the paper back into the box. The kitchen door swung open, and there stood Carol, in her bathrobe, rubbing her eyes. "Honey, are you still up? Did you get in touch with your dad?"

Holden said nothing. He just raced across the room and wrapped his mother in a long, tight hug. The kind of appreciative, loving hug he hadn't given her since he was much younger. "Oh, honey," Carol said, overcome. She glanced at the counter and saw that he had opened her present. Smiling softly, she hugged him back. "Happy birthday," she said.

In the living room, Maddie settled down in her sleeping bag, easing in quietly so she wouldn't wake her friends. It had been quite a long day, and she was exhausted. She laid her head on her pillow and closed her eyes. She wasn't sure, but just before she drifted off to sleep, she thought she heard someone say, "I love you, Mom."

THE END

About the Author

Jerry Mahoney loves books — reading them, writing them, and especially ruining them. He has written for and ruined television shows, newspapers, magazines, and the Internet. He is excited to finally be ruining something as beloved as a fairy tale. He lives in Los Angeles with his husband, Drew, and their very silly children.

About the Illustrator

Aleksei Bitskoff is an Estonian-born British illustrator. He earned a master's degree in illustration from Camberwell College of Arts in London. In 2012 he was a finalist for the Children's Choice Book Award. Aleksei lives in London with his wife and their young son.

Glossary

annihilate (uh-NYE-uh-late)—to destroy something completely

bazaar (buh-ZAHR)—a street market, especially one found in a Middle Eastern country

caravan (KAR-uh-van)—a group of people using animals or vehicles to travel together

distinct (di-STINGKT)—very clear and easy to notice

entourage (ahn-too-RAHZH)—a group of people attending or surrounding an important person

infinite (IN-fuh-nit)—without end

Neanderthal (nee-AN-der-thawl)—a species of human that lived between 35,000 and 120,000 years ago

plummet (PLUHM-it)—fall or drop straight down at high speed

primitive (PRIM-i-tiv)—at an early stage of development

scimitar (SIM-i-ter)—a short sword with a curved blade that's larger at the point

sultan (SUHL-tuhn)—an emperor or ruler of some Muslim countries

thobe (THOHB)—an ankle-length Arab piece of clothing, usually with long sleeves

Think Again

1. How do you think Chapter 1 might have played out differently if Holden had opened the present instead of throwing it in the trash? How do you think he feels when he sees the ticket?

2. When she's in *Aladdin*, Maddie learns what it's like to be a camel, a monkey, and a genie. Which one do you think was hardest for her, and why? What things could she do as a monkey that she couldn't do as a camel? Knowing how much she loves fairy tales, how do you think it made her feel to be in the story, but not as one of the main characters?

3. Holden's mom thinks hoverboards are too dangerous for her son, but she buys him a gift she thinks he'll like even more. If you were going to Holden and Maddie's birthday parties, what present would you bring each of them? Use details from the book to show why each present choice is a good one.

Clichés: Boring to Read, Fun to Ruin!

Have you ever heard of a cliché? A cliché is something that's used so often in stories that eventually, it's not fun or surprising anymore. Fairy tales are full of clichés, like wicked stepmothers or talking animals or two people falling in love at first sight. Usually, when people talk about clichés, they tell you not to use them. They say that readers are tired of them and you should try to be more original with what you write. But here's a secret: clichés can actually be a lot of fun, as long as you know how to ruin them!

In this book, Holden sings a love song to Nazeerah. You've probably seen that happen in a lot of stories. Usually, a man sings for the woman he loves, and she finds it so romantic that she plants a big old kiss on him. Right? Well, I didn't want to do it that way in my book. I knew that's what readers would expect, and if I wrote it that way, they'd probably be bored. Besides, that didn't seem to fit Holden's character at all.

So I thought about how I could do things differently. I made Holden a terrible singer. I had him do an air guitar solo, which is totally not romantic but totally something Holden would do. And I had him forget the lyrics to the love song he wanted to sing, so he had to make them up as he went along. (And of course, the words he sings end up being completely ridiculous.)

When you're writing your own stories, think of what clichés people might expect you to include. Then find ways to twist them around to make them new and surprising again. It's a great way to keep your readers on their toes, and it makes writing more fun for you, too!

Jerry

FIND MORE MAGICAL STORIES AT WWW.MYCAPSTONE.COM

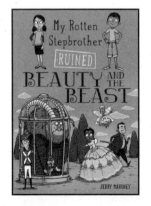

My Rotten Stepbrother RUINED BEAUTY AND THE BEAST

JERRY MAHONEY

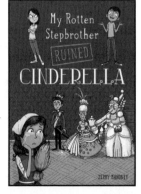

My Rotten Stepbrother RUINED CINDERELLA

JERRY MAHONEY

My Rotten Stepbrother RUINED SNOW WHITE

JERRY MAHONEY